1. URSULA K. LE GUIN, The Visionary *and*
   SCOTT R. SANDERS, Wonders Hidden

2. ANAÏS NIN, The White Blackbird *and*
   KANOKO OKAMOTO, The Tale of an Old Geisha

3. JAMES D. HOUSTON, One Can Think About Life
   After the Fish is in the Canoe *and*
   JEANNE WAKATSUKI HOUSTON, Beyond Manzanar

4. HERBERT GOLD, Stories of Misbegotten Love *and*
   DON ASHER, Angel on My Shoulder

5. RAYMOND CARVER and TESS GALLAGHER,
   Dostoevsky (The Screenplay) *and*
   URSULA K. LE GUIN, King Dog (a Screenplay)

6. EDWARD HOAGLAND, City Tales *and*
   GRETEL EHRLICH, Wyoming Stories

7. EDWARD ABBEY, Confessions of a Barbarian *and*
   JACK CURTIS, Red Knife Valley

GRETEL EHRLICH

Wyoming Stories

VOLUME VI

CAPRA PRESS
1986

For the cowboys I've ridden with—

and in memory of
Joel Grabbert
1958-1985

Printed in the United States of America.

Cover design by Francine Rudesill
Designed and typeset in Garamond by Jim Cook
SANTA BARBARA, CALIFORNIA

LIBRARY OF CONGRESS CATALOGING-IN-PUBLICATION DATA
Hoagland, Edward.
CITY TALES
(Capra back-to-back series)
Titles transcribed from individual title pages.
Contents: City Tales: The Witness. Kwan's Coney Island. The Final Fate of the Alligators; Wyoming Stories: Pinkey. Kai and Bobby. McKay. Thursdays at Snuff's.
1. Short stories, American. 2. American fiction—20th century.
I. Ehrlich, Gretel. Wyoming Stories. 1986. II. Title.
III. Title: Wyoming Stories. IV. Series: Capra back-to-back.
PS648.S5H6 1986 813'.54 85-25557
ISBN 0-88496-243-1 (pbk.)

PUBLISHED BY
CAPRA PRESS
Post Office Box 2068
Santa Barbara, Ca. 93120

CONTENTS

FOREWORD

These linked stories were written during the winter and spring of 1985 in the order of their appearance. The writing of the stories started off straightforwardly enough, but very quickly, they ballooned into a larger, longer work. One thing led to another and before I knew it I had several hundred pages in front of me and a cast of characters who would not quiet down. As such, these pieces of writing should be considered as segments of a work-in-progress.

I hope this confession will not deter you, the reader, from continuing your progress through this "back-to-back" book. The stories take place during the war years of 1942-1945. Set in the desolate mountains and valleys of northern Wyoming, they are derived from two larger, intertwined stories: one concerns the Japanese-Americans evacuated from the West Coast after Pearl Harbor to the Heart Mountain Relocation Camp; the other story concerns a family-owned cattle ranch which borders the camp as well as the nearby town of Luster, Wyoming—population, 200.

Inevitably there is a confluence between the two groups. Bobby Korematsu, the Japanese cook who has been at the Heart Ranch for twenty years walks from the ranch house to the camp one afternoon, slips through the entry gate and joins two elderly Issei gentlemen in a game of Goh. He has not seen another human being of Japanese ancestry for two decades. In another story, an evacuee becomes lost during an outing and stumbles into Snuff's Bar during a prolonged blackout. There he is befriended by a strange trio and they pass the dark hours telling the stories of their lives.

Each of the short fictions in this book have to do with the difficulties and hidden agonies of solitude, oddball western humor, and the human heart in conflict with itself. Part of the fun of attempting the short story form has been reading and rereading the masters—V.S. Pritchett, Faulkner, D.H. Lawrence, Hemingway, and eight volumes of Chekhov. I've balked at only one point—the suggestion that the short story best celebrates "the little man," as if we had, for the purpose of the form, transistorized the people around us and the characters who come, often uninvited, into our minds. It's said that Eskimos who were asked to draw maps of where they lived inked in the parts of the landscape they knew intimately much larger than the rest of the terrain. One bit of coast, one bench of ice might appear to have the scale of Australia. That's how I feel about the characters in my stories. They're bigger than life to me, as eccentric as they are ordinary, and altogether human-sized.

* * *

By strange and wonderful coincidence, the two people directly connected with this book have been my mentors and friends for a good long time. Noel Young, the publisher, has known me since I was ten and he was the young, bohemian printer in town. I loved to visit his shop. The big, black Heidelberg banged and clanked and the room was redolent with the smell of ink. Over the years, as Noel changed from printer to publisher, a variety of brilliant, tortured souls hunched over the linotype machine, dropping their cigarette ashes into the keys on late night deadlines. Noel gave me my first crack at being published in 1970, long before I started writing fulltime, and in the process, and almost unwittingly, dangled a carrot in front of me.

I'm honored to appear under the same bookcover with my friend, Edward Hoagland. What John Updike says of his essays are certainly true of his stories: they are "remarkable for their frankness, range, and pungency..." From the first time we met on a blustery October day in New York City, Ted has gone to bat for me. An invigorating, eight-year correspondence has bolstered my spirits, and in every way he has been unfailingly generous and loyal.

In this spirit of open-handedness and good cheer, may you find this small volume to your liking.

G.E.

January 21, 1986

PINKEY

ACROSS THE ROAD from the bar a calcium mine spewed pink dust that drifted across the state line into Wyoming. Two front-end loaders, a long wooden shed, and three cars on a railroad siding were dusted pink and for a mile thickets of greasewood and sagebrush, leaning south away from shouldering winds, caught the mined chalk as did the cattle who grazed there.

A sorrel horse was tied between two pickups at the bar. With her back leg cocked, her whole body looked crooked. One rein dangled straight down from the bit into the mud. Someone had written "Ride me" in the dust that covered the saddle.

Soon enough those words were obliterated by falling snow. It was snow from a storm that had hit Pinkey's camp then proceeded east across rugged grazing land, the clouds fanning out in the miles between towns like a skirt being lengthened.

"All bad weather starts here," Pinkey had said to himself. It was not winter yet and he shook his head in disgust. He had ridden through fifty years of storms, cowboying on yearling outfits in Nevada, cow-calf operations in Montana, and for the last twelve years he had worked for the young McKay. He put on his overshoes and coat, cut the wires on a bale of hay he had used as a couch all summer and fed a third of it to his mare. He looked up. He heard the drone of a plane but could see nothing. The sky like the ground was white. Yesterday it had been purely blue. One cloud had passed overhead. It was shaped like a human penis and rode the airwaves erect, pointing heavenward, Pinkey had thought, so now his usual, nuisance, morning erections, ordinarily reminding him of his solitary state, became something blessed. For a whole summer Pinkey had looked out on tall grass swinging back and forth in wind. Now snow rolled over the range. Once, after too much booze, he thought the grass was a bed of seaweed—rubbery, thick, cold—and he was trapped beneath it, bobbing for air.

He went back to bed. When he woke again he was cold. He looked outside and it occurred to him that yesterday's phallic cloud had softened and drained and come apart like cooked meat into the white smithereens falling on him as snow.

* * *

Pinkey was not in the bar where his horse was tied. Hours before he had hitched a ride into a town on the Wyoming side of the line. He cashed a paycheck saved from a summer at linecamp and bought himself new wool pants, a shirt, and a winter jacket. In the store he looked at himself in the mirror. Next to the salesman, a big Mormon man who doubled as the undertaker, Pinkey looked small. His short legs bowed, he was toothless, and from his cracked lips a line of blood drove down his chin and dripped on the floor.

He went to the bars. "Drinks for the house!" he said in each one, though "the house" rarely consisted of more than two or three old men—sheepherders or cowboys too bunged up to work—plus the bartenders who rarely drank at ten in the morning so early in what Pinkey called "the drinking year" which began when the weather turned cold.

* * *

Snow fell throughout the basin. It filled the great draws and softened tumbled breaks and the long lines of rimrock hemming the mountains above McKay's ranch shone orange. Breaking tree branches had awakened McKay. They fell against the house in sharp reports as if to remind him there was a war on. He needed none. A bad dream had awakened him earlier. He was in a hospital on the front line looking for his brothers. Room after room was filled with bodies stacked up. Their heads and limbs had been cut off and the torsoes were tied together in bundles like newspapers. That's how they were sent home.

Of three brothers, McKay was the one who could not pass an Army physical because his leg, crushed in a horse accident, was still weak and considerably shorter than the other. Naked, he limped out to the screened porch. He thought it was wind that had caused the cottonwood limbs to break, then he saw the snow. He was more legs than torso and his reedlike body was as pale and graceful as a sandhill crane's. Snow sifted sideways through the mesh and chilled him. This would bring the cows down, he thought, and wondered if Pinkey would trail them to the ranch.

There was a noise in the kitchen. Bobby Korematsu, who had come to cook at the ranch twenty years before, when McKay was seven, stuffed the woodbox of the cookstove with split pine and lit match after match until a fire roared. He set a bucket of water on the stove to boil, clacking across the floor in getas (Japanese clogs) carved the winter before. He wasn't used to cooking for just two. Before the war there had been a full house—the three boys, Pinkey, a haying or calving crew, and irrigators. Bobby had cooked three meals a day for them and no work on the ranch was appreciated more deeply.

The first night the ranch had been empty after everyone but McKay had gone to the front, McKay found Bobby in the darkened dining room crying. He was sitting on a chair whose legs had been cut down so his feet would reach the floor.

"I don't like fight. Not good for heart," he said, pounding his chest with his small hand. "See, it make me cry."

McKay pulled the elegant chair that had been his mother's so close to Bobby their knees touched but could think of nothing to say. He had lied to Bobby about his brothers, saying they were fighting in Italy when, in fact, they were in the Pacific, because after Pearl Harbor, Bobby had said, "Not possible." Another time

Bobby had seen something in the cookstove fire: his Japanese nephews slicing through the bodies of the ranch boys with swords. That night he had stood at McKay's bedroom door and said, "So ashamed," then turned quickly away.

* * *

Pinkey stood at the back of the bar called the Cactus after the owner's mule who liked beer. His bloodied lips moved as he read the new sign stuck in the corner of the mirror behind the bottles. It read: No Japs. He ordered a beer and a shot then his eyes went to the sign again. He gulped the whiskey down, then turned his back on the barman who wanted to talk. Near the door there was a pile of junk on the floor: a 410 shotgun with a broken stock, three rolls of rusted barbed wire, and a stack of bald tires.

"What's this, your dowry?" he asked the woman sitting alone at one of the booths.

"That's Jimmy Luster's stuff. Backed his wagon to the door last night and just started auctioneering things off. Said his old lady quit him so he was going to travel light for awhile."

A man wearing a red neckscarf and a hat with sweatstains circling the browband clasped an arm around Pinkey's neck.

"You should've got in on that one, Pink. Hell he would've sold you his wife," he said and laughed hoarsely.

"I bought the cigarette lighter out of his truck. Then some asshole told me he never owned one in his life," a quavering voice said from another booth. Then the speaker held the lighter gleefully in the air.

Pinkey stared at the goods on the floor. "Did Jimmy say where he was headed?"

"Didn't know," the old cowboy with the red scarf said. "See, the thing is, he just found out his kid was killed in the Pacific. Them Japs sank his ship and he was in some kinda lifeboat deal and he went plumb nuts. Jumped overboard. He couldn't swim."

Pinkey looked out the front windows of the bar. The bright morning light hurt his eyes. Fat flakes of snow were falling fast. "He'll just winterkill out there," he muttered as if talking about himself. Then he drank for the rest of the day.

* * *

The dogs dug down through five inches of new snow until they reached dirt and lay in their cone-beds with their backs to the wind. McKay brought the horses in and saddled one of them. He had decided to open the pasture gates to let the cattle, who cannot paw through snow to eat, drift in. "Open gates, cut wire, do whatever you have to during a blizzard or the cattle will walk into a draw and suffocate there," his father had always warned him.

As he rode, Heart Mountain disappeared from sight. The cloud that took it did so quickly, like a hunger, McKay thought. Now the peak broke the skin of the cloud. Nothing about it resembled a heart. It was, instead, a broken horn or a Cubist breast, as McKay's mother had once remarked. Behind it the Beartooth Mountains veered north. Forty million years ago Heart Mountain broke off from the Rockies and skidded twenty-five miles on a detachment fault to its present site. There was no other limestone in the area like it and at its base was one of the most fertile hayfields on the ranch.

As McKay rode under the limestone tusk he looked up. A half moon hooked its side. So that's how love works, he thought and chuckled out loud. He reduced his mother's geology lesson to a list of words: detachment, skidding, breast, horn, heart. As he said the words a bank of snowclouds took over every mountain west of the ranch and McKay kicked his horse into a lope. When he reached the first gate, the cattle were already waiting.

* * *

Pinkey found his dentures on the sidewalk between the Cactus and the Silver Spur Bars and lost them a third time. He couldn't walk straight. The tremor which began in his neck passed all the way down to his fingertips. A pickup full of young cowboys passed.

"Come on up to the Outlaw and we'll buy you a drink," one of the young men yelled.

A sheet of slush sprayed Pinkey's bowed legs. He looked up. A face in the cab gave him a start. It was his son. Pinkey dove into an alley. He felt sick. His empty stomach convulsed.

"Dad?"

Pinkey leaned between the brick walls of two buildings. "I thought you was up to the Outlaw," he said, trying to straighten up. He had wanted to see his son. He always wanted to see him, it was a hunger like the tug of a good woman in town, but stronger. He remembered he had promised his son he would take the cure.

"I came back to say hi. You in town for a couple of days?" the boy asked.

"You could say that," Pinkey replied dryly. "Oh Christ, I'm going to be sick, you better go."

The dry heaves scratched up through Pinkey's body and ended in his open mouth. He gasped and spit. Vincent held his father's head until the nausea passed.

Pinkey looked at his son. "How'd you get so growed up?"

The young man shrugged shyly but the wounded look in his eyes was there. Pinkey knew the look and concluded he needed one more drink before he quit. They walked to the bar.

A row of icicles fell from the eaves of the building and speared a hump of drifted snow behind their backs. They went in. Tall, lithe and slender, Vincent's broad face bore the scars of acne and from under his tall-crowned black hat two braids hung down. Pinkey ordered two beers.

"Who's your friend?" the bartender asked.

"This is my kid, Vincent," Pinkey replied proudly.

"The hell. . . ."

"His mother's Crow. You can tell because he's so tall and goodlooking."

"Yeah, but who's the father?" one of the drunks yelled from the back of the bar. The chirp in his voice sounded more like choking.

"Well I've never seen a half-breed looks like that," the bartender commented.

"That's because you've never been more than two feet out of this sonofabitchin Mormon town," Pinkey said. He stared at the bartender who busied himself wiping glasses. Pinkey stood on his toes and leaned towards the man. "We're all half-breeds," he said. "The whole goddamned country is breeds. And what the hell difference does it make? Anyone of you show me some thoroughbred blood and I'll show you a phony sonofabitch."

Pinkey stepped back from the bar. He threw a silver dollar on the counter, turned, kicked the jukebox until it lit up and played a tune, then followed Vincent to the street.

"Hey, Pinkey, do you want your change or is this my tip?" the barman asked.

When Pinkey reached the sidewalk he slipped on the ice. Vincent helped him to his feet.

"I'd better catch that ride to the ranch," Vincent mumbled. "Do you have wheels?"

"Yea. Sure," Pinkey said. The color had drained from his face again. He watched Vincent walk east along the main street. The boy moved like a wildcat, Pinkey thought. Smooth and swift and awake. Maybe he wasn't the kid's father, he thought. He brushed snow from his coat, adjusted his gray Stetson, and looked the opposite way, towards his cattle range, and walked in that direction. Stores gave way to small frame and brick houses where singed lawns burned under the snow. His hat was cocked sideways on his head and he jerked back when a dog barked at him.

Past the last house the sky closed down like a dark awning unreeled from the mountains, lowering what Pinkey thought of as infinity all the way down to the pint bottle in his back pocket from which he stopped to drink. He wiped his mouth as the liquor slid down. A skunk ran out from behind a rose bush. Pinkey howled with laughter, brushing against the red blossoms skewed with the weight of snow. The skunk zigzagged down the road, the stripe on its back crossing the white line, like crossing his t's, Pinkey thought, and so came to assume that the highway would spell out messages for him if he walked far enough along its edge.

Two dogs came out from behind the Mormon church and trotted at Pinkey's heels. Pinkey turned and whistled to them. For twelve years he had trained the stockdogs at McKay's ranch never addressing them in a voice louder than a whisper. He felt good. He'd wanted company and now he had dogs. He looked at the sky. The clouds had curdled and thickened. He thought of the storm as the product of the penis cloud he'd seen the day before. It had knocked up some old gal and now there was this.

From a distance a red and white graintruck approached the trio. The dogs sprinted ahead, leaping up and changing directions midair to chase the truck. Pinkey watched them. Another truck followed and the dogs repeated their act. Pinkey crouched down and followed the action with his head. He thought he'd give it a try. When the third truck came he ran alongside it and barked. After ten yards he stopped and stood up, puffing, while the dogs jumped up and down in delight. For a long time there were no other vehicles on the road. The trio waited. Wind blew snow into Pinkey's face so he and the dogs clambered down into the borrow pit. Like swimmers, they waded through tall grass, their feet rolling over the tops of beer bottles as they walked.

A car appeared. Pinkey crawled up to the road, clutching bunchgrass as he climbed. The headlights bore down on him. "You jacklightin' sonofabitch," he yelled. The lights were on him like crossed eyes. He didn't know where to look. He crouched down, barking in unison with the dogs, a magnificent high-pitched crooning cut off suddenly by a *whomp*. The car shuddered, fishtailed, and slid to a stop. A cyclone fence on the far side of the borrow pit vibrated. Pinkey sprawled against the fence and moaned. The driver of the car ran to the collapsed figure.

"God almighty, mister. . . are you. . . ?"

Pinkey looked up. The man crouching over him had dark eyes. Like Vincent's. Was this Vincent? No. Then Pinkey remembered why he had come to town that day. It was Vincent's birthday.

"You killed me, you sonofabitch," Pinkey said.

The driver dropped to his knees and began sobbing.

"Well hell, I ain't really dead," Pinkey said and grinned.

The driver wiped his nose.

"Don't just stare at me. Take me to the hospital. I think my leg's busted."

The man pulled his jacket off and spread it across Pinkey's chest. "I'm sorry, man. I'm really sorry."

"Oh shutup," Pinkey said and when he spoke, his toothless gums caught the glint of headlights from an oncoming truck.

* * *

McKay drew out a deck of cards thrown loosely in a drawer with the silverware. He had lost seventy-nine games of gin rummy to Bobby in the year 1942 and expected to lose this one. Bobby pushed the worn scorecard across the oilcloth while McKay shuffled and dealt. A truck pulled into the yard. McKay looked at his hand quickly while pushing his chair back to stand up.

"Good god. If this ain't a cobbled up mess. How am I ever going to win a game?"

"Just clean up mess," Bobby said wryly.

Madeleine stood in the doorway. Snow blew into the room and for a moment McKay was mesmerized by the way it hit the tip of her nose and dissolved on her cheeks.

"Pinkey's dead," she said flatly.

"You can't kill that sonofabitch," McKay said. Then a look of alarm came over his face. "Are you sure?"

"No. But you better go to the hospital. That's where they were taking him."

McKay touched Madeleine's shoulder and was gone.

Two women rolled Pinkey into the x-ray room on a gurney. He lay back, his hands folded behind his head.

"Do you want to take my pants off now or later?" he asked the two nurses and winked. They smiled and said nothing.

The transfer to the examining table proceeded with difficulty. Pinkey refused to help. On the contrary, he relaxed further, a deadweight for the two women. McKay burst in. With one motion he lifted his hired hand to the table.

"For god's sake, Pinkey . . ."

Pinkey gave McKay a grin. "Where's the cards, the flowers, the candy?"

"Oh, they're just flooding in," McKay said sarcastically.

Pinkey turned to the nurses. "Are you going to strip me now?" he asked.

"Sorry old man. Maybe another time," the heavier of the two replied. Then she split the seam of his trousers with a razor.

"Stop it! My new pants!" Pinkey howled.

"Just slap the sonofabitch," McKay said and motioned to the nurse to continue cutting.

* * *

The hospital let Pinkey sleep it off in the vacant labor room for no extra charge. He slept until the pain in his leg woke him. When he opened his eyes the walls of the room folded down around him and spun. He closed them again. The beads of darkness under his lids spun too, zooming backwards then bursting against some inward wall, the color of garnets. He felt a terrible weight in his body. Maybe they put a body cast on with my arms inside so I can't hold a bottle, he thought. He tried to move his arms and swung himself into the black room until he hit something and there was a crash. Then the sickly weight pulled him down.

A switch clicked and the room filled with light like a lung.

"Did we fall out of bed?" a big woman in white asked. She helped Pinkey up.

"I guess my wings broke," he said.

"Up we go. Now, we'll put these sides up so we don't try to fly again."

Pinkey felt the hard bed under him again. When the nurse's face came close he thought he heard a terrible roar like snow falling from a roof. Then the room was black again. He tried to lie still but his shoulders twitched and his whole body splintered like rotten wood. He saw a bottle somewhere in front of him and when he reached for it, it broke, but the whiskey wouldn't spill. It stood up as if frozen, then all at once, shattered. His arms lengthened, reaching for it. He tried to think of why the need came on him. Then his arms were fifty yards long, his hands like tiny knobs and still he could touch nothing and the need grew, a malevolent bloom.

* * *

"You havin' a baby or do you want to go home?" McKay asked throwing light into the room.

Pinkey sat up and looked around. "Am I dead?"

"How the hell do I know, I ain't the doctor."

"What time is it?" Pinkey asked.

"Morning. And if we don't get home pretty soon, we'll be snowed out for the winter."

"Sounds good to me," Pinkey said. He felt clear-headed suddenly and slid off the bed, hopping on one leg.

McKay handed him the crutches. "God, if you don't look like a jackrabbit."

* * *

A fog swallowed the road ahead of McKay's pickup and mixed with steam off the river. They drove north in the dark. Ahead the sky began to clear.

"What'd you have to go and get drunk for?" McKay asked. He was tired.

"That's why."

"What's why?"

"Because I'm tired of having reasons. Why can't a man just go and do stuff?"

"Well you ain't going to be doing much with that thing on your leg."

From out of the dark a roadsign loomed: WELCOME TO BIG SKY COUNTRY—MONTANA. A horse ran in front of the truck. McKay swerved hard.

"Hey. That's my mare," Pinkey shouted and pointed at the horse now saddleless, eating what McKay referred to as "government feed" which meant the grass on the side of the highway.

The truck skidded to a halt. Pinkey looked. He could see the blurred outline of the calcium plant. A half moon shot up out of empty railroad cars and stars shone like pinholes in ice. Across the road his saddle had been dumped on end under the bar sign which pulsed, throwing a bloody pool on the snow every second or so. Dawn broke as pink and dry as calcium dust. Though Pinkey knew the sight had something to do with how the future becomes the present and the present the future, he still felt like a banty rooster crowing at first light, not caring or knowing what it portended.

McKay backed the pickup to a sidehill and loaded the mare. Pinkey rolled down his window. "I named her Eleanor, for Eleanor Roosevelt," he said.

McKay slapped the horse on the rump and she jumped in. The

top of her back steamed where snow had melted and the ice hanging in her mane clanged together like a crystal chandelier.

McKay turned the truck around and they drove south. Now the sign read: WELCOME TO BIG WONDERFUL WYOMING. Pinkey inspected his cast as if seeing it for the first time. He drummed on it here and there and discovered some of the plaster was still wet.

"Don't you worry about them cows," he said. "I left them on auto pilot. And don't worry about this cast either. We'll cut her off in a couple of weeks and I'll be good as new."

A smile came over McKay's face but the old man didn't see it. They drove in silence. Pinkey pulled his coat tightly around him. He cradled his head with a gloved hand and a wheezing snore came from his half-opened mouth and filled the cab with a sound that reminded McKay of peace.

The truck bumped along the ungraded ranch road. McKay stopped once to check a mudhole and when he climbed back in, he looked at the old cowboy with affection. In his sleep, Pinkey felt McKay's eyes on him. It was like heat penetrating his heavy lids. He wanted to laugh but his body made no sound.

KAI AND BOBBY

HE LAY ACROSS the bed with only a shirt on. It was late and it was raining again. After Li made love to him she rested her head on his stomach.

"You nervous. Everything noisy in there," she said.

Kai shifted, laughing, and pulled one knee up. Then he reached over and lit a cigarette. The room smelled of green vegetables and cooking oil. Li climbed off the bed.

"Here," she said, pinning a badge to Kai's shirt. She kissed his chest. The noise of the city wallowed in the room, a mechanical gargling of horns, rain, and engines. On the fire escape the potted chrysanthemum Kai had given to Li on her birthday tossed about in the wind. Kai contemplated the badge. He ground the butt of his cigarette out until it looked like a pig's flared snout, then clasped Li's head tightly in the crook of his arm. Her hair shone like the stalks of black bamboo. He rolled her from side to side, his arms locked across the small of her back, his legs entwined with hers until she wriggled away from him. He grabbed her again and pinned her down with a wrestler's hold on her neck.

"Hello," he said.

Li smiled. Her small swimmer's kicks knocked against his shins, then she went limp and floated towards him. Kai dropped heavily beside her. A coolness shifted through his body. Li examined his face.

"Who are you?" she said.

* * *

That was a Thursday in September of 1942. Two days later Kai and his parents were on a train. All through the cars he could see only black hair, dark eyes, the sound of a language his parents had forbidden him to learn. The journal he began keeping that day was a way of steadying himself against drastic change. The lullaby rocking on traintracks felt deathly to him. He dreamed the tracks were his arms. He was holding Li. The heavy cars rolled over them.

When Kai woke his arms were asleep. He had been sitting on his hands. Out the train window the desert looked like the palm of a hand on which life had drawn no lines.

In San Francisco Jimmy Wong, Li's older brother by twelve years, had burst into their room.

"No more Chinese women for you," he'd said and winked at Kai. He handed Kai a final edition of the Chronicle. It read: ALL JAPS MUST GO!

Jimmy turned solemn. He plunked down on the bed and

looked out the window. The building across the street that housed the dumpling shop and the Mah Jong room was dark. A fire escape hung tentatively to its side and a green dragon, used in the New Year's parade, lay unfurled against three upstairs windows.

Jimmy whispered: "You stay here. Marry Li. Keep go to college. Change from great Japanese scholar to great Chinaman."

As he spoke the rain intensified and enclosed the streets of Chinatown like sea lanes in a fog that led to places no one in that room knew.

Kai unpinned the badge and twirled it between his fingers. the safety pin pricked his thumb. A drop of blood appeared. Li held his thumb up and licked the blood away. Kai would remember her diminuitiveness, standing naked in that noisy room, he would remember the tart taste of her skin.

He pulled his hand away from her and flung it over his head in a mocking backstroke as if to swim from intimacy. She opened the window. Cold rain blew in. She pulled the potted plant whose heavy white blossoms were bent completely over into the room.

* * *

Like a great elastic band the train stretched Kai away from that magnetic point on the compass. In his journal he wrote:

> Slowly the train steamed out of Berkeley. As I looked out the window I could see the green hills dotted with houses. Strange but I hadn't noticed the soft greeness before. I remembered that in the hurried retreat I had left my room in turmoil. An Issei would have been

ashamed to leave the place in less than perfect order
so as not to betray any confusion in his mind.

That last night Kai had waited for sunrise in an all-night upstairs tea shop. There was a curfew for "all people of Japanese ancestry" and it would have been dangerous for him to walk the streets after dark. At nine he boarded the ferry to Richmond. He hadn't seen his parents for two years. The man at the ticket office, a Filipino, had hesitated before giving Kai passage.

"He didn't say anything. He just looked at me and held onto that stub," Kai told his father after their strained, awkward greeting. Later, alone in the kitchen with his mother, she told Kai that his father hadn't recognized him at first.

"Can you imagine?" she said. Then, "He's getting more and more like that."

In the living room Mr. Nagouchi bent towards the big radio. It lit his face like a jack o'lantern. Kai's mother stirred scallions into broth, shoyu, and sake, then the eggs and eel.

"I don't eat this food very often anymore," Kai said.

"Oh, this is special for you. Unagi donburi. You always liked it," she said, though Kai could remember liking no such thing.

After lunch Kai and his father drove to town. Mr. Nagouchi wanted to show his son the store.

"How's business been going, Pop?"

Mr. Nagouchi grunted. "No good now." It was a Wednesday but Japantown was deserted. Mr. Nagouchi unlocked the door. It was a triangular building at the end of a block flanked by two narrow streets. When Kai walked up and down the aisles the floorboards squeaked. He looked at shelves of tools—planers, chisels, Japanese saws, and a ceiling-high stack of black twine rolled into balls. In another aisle were rice cookers, bamboo water ladles, brass teapots, packets of seed, and a penny jar full of bubble gum.

Mr. Nagouchi took his place behind the counter for the last time. Behind his head was the business license he'd framed austerely in black and next to it, a photograph of the great Buddha at Nara.

"For god's sake, pop, take that down. Have Mom bring the Navy pictures or something," Kai said.

Mr. Nagouchi stood motionless. The son he had sent away to be raised as a scholar was giving him orders the way American boys do. Kai inserted a penny into the jar and popped a jaw breaker into his mouth. When his father struggled with a lock at the back door, Kai helped him. Finally the door swung open. Instead of the street, there was a garden—a tiny miniaturized place with stepping stones, mossy banks, a stone water basin, three flowering shrubs, and against a tall fence, a thicket of black bamboo.

"I sold the business yesterday," Kai's father said solemnly. "Seven hundred. The car too. But I didn't show them this."

Kai spit his gum into his hand and stared at the massive block of stone under his feet. Already the moss had begun to grow beyond its borders. Across the street a bell in the Buddhist temple rang. Then Kai heard glass breaking. He looked around. Mr. Nagouchi had broken a picture frame and held a match to the photograph of the Buddha at Nara. The glossy paper lifted and curled towards the old man and became ash.

They locked the store and got in the Studebaker. Sometimes the horn stuck and Mr. Nagouchi had to lift the hood and pinch a certain wire, but not today. They glided through empty streets. Their first night of evacuation would be spent at a racetrack in converted horsestalls. The idea amused Kai at first and he thought of bringing a rake from the store for the manure, but changed his mind.

"Seabiscuit, here we come," he said, though quietly so his father would not hear.

* * *

The train lurched to a stop. There was no town. Only a water tank and a switchbox. Kai closed his journal and ran to the train door. He jumped down to the wooden platform, tilted his head back and inhaled dry air deeply. Two army soldiers eyed him. They had guns. Steam from the train's engine hissed and the great trunk that was the water hose swung against the black cab. Ahead Kai could see the Rocky Mountains. Snow covered the higher peaks. "Bring clothes suited to pioneer life," they had been advised. The thought made Kai chuckle.

A handsome couple joined Kai on the platform. They introduced themselves as Will Okubo and Mariko Abé. They had been living in Paris. She was a painter. Kai didn't catch what Will Okubo said about himself. He was tall, lean, and pale and used a cigarette holder. His khaki pants were held up by suspenders and he sported a white beret. Some pioneer, Kai thought. Mariko's hair looked like a raven's wing. She pursed her lips when she listened and fastened her wild eyes on one thing, then another, as if to keep the fragments whole in her mind.

An "all-aboard" sounded. The trio put out their cigarettes and climbed on the train. In the aisle they nodded to one another and parted. Kai looked in on his parents. They had slept through the stop. His mother's mouth was open and his father's head was tucked against his shoulder the way a bird sleeps and his glasses hung crookedly from his nose. Kai began a letter:

Dear Li,

Can you imagine how I feel? I don't even know myself. A little while ago a wave of loneliness came over me like nothing I've felt before. Then I met two interesting people at a stop in the middle of nowhere. In fact, I don't know where we are. They could be taking us to hell, for all I know. So I keep trying to think of this ridiculous lapse in the democratic process as an adventure. Maybe that's just being naive.

Tell Jimmy we've been following a river called the Virgin River all afternoon, and it runs red. Can you beat that? Otherwise it's awfully desolate out here. When we left the Assembly Center I saw a man with his arms stuck through the fence, holding his girlfriend, and it made me think of you. But for the time being, I'm a family man. Isn't that funny after all those years as an orphan. Mom and Pop are awfully scared and sad. I've been trying to make the trip comfortable for them but it's hard. Some of this American food they've been eating has made them sick. They'd never had a hamburger before. After all those years in Richmond. By the way, I told them about you.

> Pop has hardly said a word since he closed up the store. It's heartbreaking. I can't believe I won't be going to school again for a long time and in the evenings, coming to you.
>
> We heard that at another camp someone sent a box of oranges with a sword inside. A Nisei ran with it and the MP's shot him dead. They must be taking lessons from Hitler.
>
> I guess I'll try to get some sleep now. I feel so strange being apart from you. It's like I have a big hole in my back that grows bigger and bigger where my heart has flown out and travels towards you.
>
> love, Kai

He closed his journal and slept. Not long afterwards and still in the dark, the train, with its five hundred bewildered passengers, reached Heart Mountain Relocation Camp, a cluster of buildings on a barren plain surrounded by mountains and low hills.

After several hours of confusion the families found their way to the barracks and began to settle in. Kai and his parents were assigned an apartment next door to Mariko, Will Okubo, and Mr. Abé. At first Kai's father sat on his suitcase and could not be moved. Then he started crying. Finally Kai and Will lifted the old man to his feet and escorted him to his new home.

Afterwards the two young men had a smoke outside. The tar papered barracks behind them shuddered each time the wind gusted. First light came, then the sun rode the sidehills and sage-covered bench above them. They saw a little bunch of antelope and a family of deer. Already the grass had turned fawn-colored and the does and fawns had begun to turn dark. A coyote threaded his way along a fenceline towards Heart Mountain. Its long fur was silver.

Will's cigarette burned quickly to the edge of its ivory holder. He was shivering. Kai looked at him, then gave him his jacket. On the ridge above the Camp a line of cattle filed by. A blackbird rode the back of one bull and a lone rider brought up the rear of the procession.

"Do you think he sees us?" Will asked.

Kai shrugged and strained to decipher the face of the man who soon rode out of sight. When the sun reached the Camp it threw a grillwork of fence shadows across Will and Kai and the shadows of the guard towers leaned sideways, penetrating the barracks and moving across the beds of those who dove fitfully into sleep.

"Trés formidable, huh?" Will said.

Kai threw his cigarette on the dry ground.

"God, there's nothing here," he said and smiled incredulously.

* * *

The handrail over the footbridge to Bobby's cabin was made of barbed wire. Each evening when the footing was slick from dew or ice he steadied himself on it the way he had held the ship's railing when he made the crossing to America forty-five years ago. He cut his hands on the wire only twice: once, when he heard McKay's sobs of grief on hearing his parents were dead, and again, the night the electricity for the hastily constructed relocation camp was turned on and the southern horizon of the ranch was struck with light.

Bobby had heard the trains pull in since August. He was not used to noises on the ranch other than the ones made by weaned calves or haying machines or meadowlarks. Too far away to pick out distinct human voices, there was only a low roar that would increase in volume as the camp grew to 10,000 souls and Bobby would remark that it was the biggest city he had seen since leaving his parents' kimono store near the crowded wharves of Osaka.

When Bobby lit the cookstove that September morning a wasp, still comatose from last night's hard frost, burned to a crisp on the back lid. Pinkey, the only hired hand left on the ranch since the war had begun, ate the breakfast Bobby made for him. A purple bruise had flowered on his left cheek since the accident and he was having trouble negotiating his way on crutches. All the time he mouthed his pancakes Bobby thought about wasps and snow. They were part of a long seasonal progression linked and curving through time like the deer spine he had found draped gracefully on a rock outside his cabin door. Rain, flies, and mud swallows were followed by heat, mosquitoes, and deerflies, followed by rainlessness, grasshoppers, and rattlesnakes, then, as a last gasp before the glittering apocalypse of winter, wasps and the first snows.

Of Osaka Bobby remembered little. Only interminable rain, wharf rats, and the bright foliage of kimonos above his bed: colors like green winter melons and pale crysanthemums half lost in dark silk folds.

Four buckets of water came to a boil on the cookstove. Bobby poured them into a big galvanized tub on the floor. Naked except for the cast which ended just below the knee and which he referred to as "that half-mast sonofabitch," Pinkey looked round and cherubic and insisted on bathing with his hat on. Bobby tested the water with his little finger.

"Hey, this ain't baby formula we're cookin' up is it?"

Bobby shook his head.

"How the hell do I get in?"

Bobby offered his shoulder. With a great awkward effort Pinkey lunged over the side of the tub with his broken leg airborne and eased himself into the water. Then, with a magician's flourish, he pulled a packet of bubble bath from under his hat and poured it in.

In Osaka there had been the baths—dark, echoing, humid places with tile floors and the rubbery bodies of sailors and working men. Bobby thought about the uniformed men who had come to the ranch the week before. McKay, who was on horseback, stopped them before they reached the house. The one man had a crewcut, a cactus stand of hair, and the other had long fingers that turned up at the end like those of wealthy men who had never dug a posthole or roped a calf. McKay had sat his horse stiffly and when the strangers got back into their Army car he pulled his hat down and wheeled the horse to the barn.

There was another visitor that night. McKay found Madeleine sitting on the steps of the screened porch. Her head was in her arms and snow was collecting in the brim of her hat. She had received a telegram. Her husband, Henry, had been taken prisoner of war, not in Germany as Bobby had been told, but in Japan. Later she and McKay came into the kitchen.

"What will they do to him?" she asked Bobby, who, instead of replying, fled the room.

Pinkey hummed as he washed behind his ears. He let his hands float on top of the water and gathered bubbles towards his chest until he had amassed two prodigious breasts. When they dissolved Bobby helped him out of the tub. Pinkey hopped to a chair and began to dry himself—face, neck, under his arms, his legs and balls. When he looked up he found Bobby staring at him.

"You think I bad now? Should go to Camp with other Japanese?" Bobby asked.

Pinkey stopped dabbing. He felt uneasy. A sadness came forward from somewhere behind or below the optic nerve in his eye and poured itself around the black iris until the whole face softened. Finally Pinkey spoke.

"You and I've been on this outfit a long time and I figure we're just about the same man. We both come away from home when we was kids and we know how to live high on the hog and how to survive too. And we know what makes people tick because they ain't no different than the coyotes or that horse herd out there and we damn sure have to get along with them to survive. And we're both gettin' old. And under this is just an ol' boneyard, ain't it? Just a bunch of bones and once they're scattered on the ground who will know which is mine and which is yours and which is the coyotes?"

Bobby let his small body down on the chair. His feet swung under him because they did not touch the floor. Then he looked at

Pinkey and dug into his pocket and pulled carefully folded news clippings out and gave them to the old cowboy. Pinkey handed them back.

"You read them. I ain't got my glasses on."

Bobby read: "PARK COUNTY SAYS NO TO JAPS HERE" "A JAP IS A JAP".

Pinkey sat motionless in the chair. Bath water had dripped around his feet. Then he held up one of his crutches and swung it like a baseball bat as though fighting off invisible demons in the air.

Bobby finished the ranch chores early. Pinkey had fallen asleep by the fire and Bobby was careful not to wake him. In the hallway he pulled his boots on then bundled up in a wool coat. He left the house by the kitchen door and walked south accompanied by two Red Heelers who would not stay home. Once, where the road became the creek and the creek the road, Bobby thought about how easily one thing can become another, how chameleon and insubstantial we are. By mid-afternoon he had reached the Heart Mountain Camp.

* * *

Three young Nisei boys goosestepped by the guardhouse and saluted. "Heil, Hitler," they boomed out, then broke into a run. Momentarily distracted, the MP's let Bobby through the gate. The two red dogs stayed on the other side of the fence and whined.

Bobby walked past rows and rows of block housing. At the end of each building men and women picked through scraps of lumber. From the shower rooms a tall woman in a silk robe ran along a muddy walkway. Her wet hair had turned white with frost. A baby cried. Plumes of smoke churned from each building and merged with snowclouds. When he thought he might meet someone he knew, some member of his family perhaps, his heart drummed and his pulse felt ropey and he imagined the blood running through him was yellow sap. He walked and walked like an insomniac.

As evening came on he could see into the living quarters. The woman he had seen in the silk robe tousled her hair in front of a wood stove. An emaciated young man lay on a bed behind her. He blew smoke rings in the air and spoke French, not English or Japanese. Through another window Bobby saw an old man crying into a white handkerchief, three teenage girls giggling over a magazine, and a young man standing at the window writing in a journal and smoking. Then he came on three old men hunched over a Goh board. They spoke to one another in Japanese. Bobby listened. He gargled the familiar words in his mouth. The sounds hit the back of his teeth but they no longer carried any meaning. Bobby was shocked to find he had forgotten so much. The words fluttered, landing nowhere. But he remembered Goh, and the snap of white and black stones on wood went off inside him like switches.

It was dark. Bobby's dogs lay curled against each other at the sentry gate. A half moon came and went behind clouds and Heart Mountain brightened and darkened accordingly. An MP with a Coke in his hand came to the guardhouse door.

"Pass please."

"No live here. . . . I'm cook for twenty years at Heart Ranch," Bobby said and pointed upcountry.

The MP turned to his partner. "We have another joker out here."

"What's your name, boy?"

"I'm not boy. Old enough to be your grandfather."

The soldiers laughed. On the hill behind them a family of coyotes began yipping. Bobby's dogs growled and went after them. When Bobby tried to call them back, they wouldn't come.

"Who are you then?" the soldier asked.

Bobby gave his name. He looked in the direction of the ranch but could see no lights. The Big Dipper bent its elbow down where the ranch should have been. He thought of the trains he had seen coming in, full of Nisei and Issei, the "yellow peril," and how those trains travelled on track he had helped build, and how they were bringing everything he had forgotten he was back to him.

The soldiers motioned Bobby into the guardhouse. They had been playing checkers. Bobby sat down and folded his hands. The coyotes had stopped howling and it was quiet. A terrible, raw quiet. Then a voice said Bobby's name. He stood up and went to the door and a short ruddy man wearing a gray Stetson cocked sideways on his head and propelling himself forward on crutches appeared.

McKAY

"The weather spirit is blowing the storm out,
the weather spirit is driving the weeping snow away over
the earth, and the helpless storm-child Narsuk shakes the
lungs of the air with his weeping."

—COOPER ESKIMO

WHEN MCKAY WOKE there was a dead rooster on the floor. He sat up with a start because he was in the wrong bedroom. He picked up the bird. At first he didn't know how it had landed there, then he remembered the cockfight the night before. The rooster was light in his hands. Its scarlet comb had been clipped short and at the back of each yellow foot a sharpened spur protruded, white as a woman's fingernail.

McKay stood and the room went black. There was no heat in that part of the house and he pulled on his long underwear quickly. As he straightened the bed he caught sight of himself in the mirror: the one side of his face looked old, the eye twitched and the soft flesh under the eye was gray as if ash had been smeared there; the other side, the bright side, looked childlike, the way one corner of the mouth was pulled down, and the split face was topped by one insouciant tumble of blond hair.

He called for Bobby, the cook, but no one answered. It was the third day of a savage, unseasonal storm. During the night a cloud shaped like an appendix had burst, dropping its white cargo like poison, and wind had violated the one tree. Its green topknot exploded and dropped branches into the arms of lower limbs like bodies being carried home from war.

The house had never seemed so quiet. When McKay looked down into the living room from the balcony he saw that everything was covered with snow. In front of each window and door were duncecaps of white. Some had toppled sideways. Wind had sprayed snow over furniture, into the black corners of the fireplace, and across the Navajo rugs on the floor.

McKay hobbled down the stairs. Today was the thirteenth anniversary of his parents' death. They had drowned when their car rolled into an irrigation canal. He picked up their silver-framed photograph taken the day they died. His mother was bundled in a fur coat. Her gray eyes sparkled and she was smiling at McKay's father whose black hair stood on end. It had been windy. He had the hurt, far-off look of someone who only finds happiness elsewhere.

McKay went to the kitchen and stoked the cookstove. Outside wind had swept the ground almost free of snow. Only the buildings and fencelines were drifted. He pulled a stool up and turned the radio on. Each morning McKay braced himself for bad news, expecting to hear his brothers' names on the casualty list. Instead, there was no news at all.

After his brothers left to go to war the rooms of the house felt too big and the huge pasture McKay rode to check cows looked like the moon. The sky went gray as if the planet had turned from the sun, averting its face. Sometimes McKay imagined one of the bombs had gone astray and floated alongside him. His loneliness took on a metallic glare—metal flying fast. The snowdrifts at the doors pressed at him and the ungodly stillness roared.

* * *

The morning of the cockfight McKay rode out through the west gate towards sheepcamp where he was to meet his neighbor, Madeleine. It was shipping day. The ranchers had gathered their cattle and trailed them to sorting corrals where they would be shipped by rail to Omaha. On the way McKay saw seven cow elk on the flank of Heart Mountain. A young bull bugled, his low whistle ascending sharply until air caught at the entrance to his throat, then he gave out three seal-like, grunting cries. The bull approached a cow. He thrust a knee between her back legs and horned her, tilting his branching antlers into her rump. She jumped and ran. He pursued her, lifting his nose in the air to inhale the full brunt of her sexual fragrance.

McKay dropped down the slope to a creekbed and entered a canyon. It narrowed quickly. The straight-up red walls hemmed him in. Far above, thin pine trees swan-necked out from cracks in the rock, then grew straight towards the sky. Occasionally, three foot long icicles dropped, taking the air like harpoons. One arced past the horse's nose then broke like crystal stemware across the trail. McKay watched the tracks in front of his horse: deer, elk, rabbit, bird, and bobcat. They looked like music to him, a skating, hopping, notational scrawl left behind by players who had gone elsewhere.

At the far end the canyon widened and McKay rode to Raoul's camp. Madeleine wasn't there. He warmed himself by the tiny cookstove inside the wagon. On the bed was a Bible and a loaded rifle. He remembered the night he and Raoul had been snowed in together. They shared the high, built-in bed across the back of the wagon. The old sheepherder lit a candle and their shadows blossomed on the rounded ceiling. That was the night he told McKay about the hurricane.

"The *tormenta*—that is what we called the hurricane in Mexico. She comes on so fast, see. . . sand blowing so hard I can't see nothing. Then it grows dark and it rains. Our village is on a hill and all of us are crowding together praying. We hear a big roar, like God himself talking, and we run out to see what has happened. It is the hill falling. It is water running everywhere. This woman, she is standing next to me, holding her baby. The water comes and sweeps that baby right out of her arms. . . then she goes too. Just like that—all that creation—pufff. Then I *knew* it was God talking. In the morning I see the whole village is gone. Well then, what am I to do? So I walk all the way to La Paz. Three days I am walking. When I get there I meet others just like me—who have come from nothing, who have nothing. But pretty soon we find jobs. And the man whose wife was washed away, he meets another woman and starts his life all over again. In no time he is happy. You think is crazy? But life is like that. *La vida es muy historica, no?*"

Then Raoul blew out the candle and McKay rolled onto his side, away from the old man, and pretended to sleep.

* * *

McKay rode on following two sets of horsetracks across a ridge, down into a coulee. Two eagles circled. He saw Madeleine and Raoul digging sheep out of a snowdrift that had curled back at the top like an upper lip sneering. McKay stepped off his horse.

"I guess they just gave up and suffocated," Madeleine said, handing McKay the back legs of two bloated ewes. When they dragged the last of seven dead sheep from the drift it collapsed into a white ruin like the cities of Europe that had been destroyed.

Raoul emerged from the timber with five crosses made from pine twigs tied at the center with bits of string. He kneeled in front of the dead sheep and planted the crosses in the snow.

Afterwards Madeleine and McKay rode towards town. They had been childhood friends, then lovers. By the time she surrendered her virginity to him and his to her in a dry irrigation ditch wrapped in a canvas dam that smelled of mildew, they had already worked cattle, roped, and ridden colts together and continued to do so. They had been born on the same day in the same hospital, McKay in the delivery room and Madeleine in the labor room, there being only one of each in the small country hospital, and when she came home after four years of college with a husband on her arm McKay felt as welcoming to the man as he did betrayed.

They rode for a time without talking. McKay liked the way she sat a horse: she took a deep seat and kept a light hand. A fresh set of clouds billowed and leapfrogged across the face of Heart Mountain. They stopped for lunch though McKay wasn't hungry. He'd finally understood the arbitrariness of life since the War had begun: it was vicarious shell-shock—black dreams, trembling, an absence of the small lusts.

He unrolled his yellow slicker and laid it across an outcropping of rock. From their perch he and Madeleine could see a corner of the Relocation Camp. McKay uncorked his flask and offered it to Madeleine. She took a swallow and wiped her mouth. It had been a week since she had heard her husband, Henry, had been taken prisoner of war in Japan.

McKay unwrapped a sandwich for her. She watched as he fed his to his dog.

"What are you thinking about?" she asked. She always asked the questions she wanted someone to ask her.

"Henry," McKay said.

"Are you thinking well of him?"

"That's a mean thing to say," McKay said and looked at her.

"Maybe he's dead, anyway," she said bitterly.

Down at the Camp they heard roosters crowing and the lines of a baseball diamond showed through melting snow. McKay leaned back on the rock and closed his eyes.

"Are you sure you want to ride to Omaha with the cattle?" he asked sleepily.

"Are you worried about me?"

"Hell no. It just means I'll be short-handed for a week."

"Thanks," she said and mussed his hair playfully. He looked at her. The gray light made her eyes turn violet.

"I'll miss you," she said almost inaudibly.

He turned towards her. Under the hat her long hair was tucked behind an ear whose bony convolutions shone, inviting him to fall in there. A tumbling rock startled them. McKay smiled his crooked, mischievious smile.

"I think you were the first person I saw when I was born," he said.

* * *

The shipping corrals loomed back against the sky and everywhere there was great commotion. Weaned calves bawled for their mothers, yardmen snapped bullwhips over the backs of steers, cowboys on horseback pushed a pen-full of heifers down a wide alley to a loading chute. Waiting boxcars thumped forward as each was loaded.

For the rest of the day McKay and Madeleine worked the chute. They pushed steers up the slippery ramp, sometimes hoisting them bodily. Some fell and had to be righted, others turned so they were facing backwards in the chute. Madeleine and McKay were kicked and tromped, their pantlegs green with manure. Falling snow piled up in their hatbrims as they worked.

When the door of the last cattle car rolled shut, Madeleine unsaddled her horse and let him drink and roll in an empty pen.

The windows of the cafe across the road had steamed up and the lights looked like an ornament against so much desolate land. She grabbed McKay's arm and drew him towards her. Just then the yardlights came on and shadows from the sorting corrals made bars across her face.

McKay remembered the night the telegram about Henry had come. He had urged Madeleine to stay the night at the ranch. Bobby made a bed in an upstairs room and led her the length of the balcony with a kerosene lamp. Once again their twin lives were stacked like a double entendre. He felt her presence in the house that night as some kind of tenderness swelling. It filled him and somehow he was lifted up through the ceiling to her bed.

Now her teeth chattered. Snow blew in a crossfire between them. McKay closed his eyes. It seemed they were naked and he was moving in and out of her like a furred animal, long and warm and sweet, standing on his hind legs. To be inside her he had to hitch his whole body up and when he came or thought he had come, water rushed by the narrow bones in his face and he heard sheets of ice cracking. Then he was cold as if he had been without clothes all winter. The air was dry. The dryness crackled between them and a spark popped when he finally touched her arm.

Now McKay clasped Madeleine's arm so tightly his knuckles turned white. He didn't know if he was shaking her or if the cold in her body was shaking him, or if, in stopping her embrace he had intended to pull her against him. Her amythyst eyes shone.

"I'm sorry," she said, and the flush on her cheeks travelled sideways to her ears.

* * *

McKay carried his dog into the cafe. It was hot inside and the floor was greasy with melted snow and mud. He swung onto a stool at the long counter. The dog curled up at his feet and began snoring. The room was full with men. Those who weren't eating stood behind those who were and each time the door swung open the noise inside the cafe redoubled with the sound of bawling calves.

"McKay?" Carol Lyman stood in front of the young rancher, a coffee pot suspended in air. He nodded. She poured, then turned, catching a glimpse of herself in the mirror, and primped her brittle hair.

"And I'll have a piece of that pie," McKay said.

She slid a plate towards him.

"And the little shit probably wants a hamburger," he said indicating the dog on the floor.

"With everything?"

"No onions," he said and winked at her.

More bodies crowded in behind McKay, men he had known all his life, men his father's age, bundled in long wool coats and tall boots.

"I'll have a whiskey and ditch of some of that pie," one of them shouted.

"Which kind?"

"I don't care. Just one of them round ones," he said and broke into laughter.

Two old cowboys shouldered in behind McKay and set their cups on the counter to be refilled.

". . . Hell no, I was tied hard and fast and when that ol' bull hit the end of the rope he whipped around. . ."

Carol Lyman returned with the pie.

"Where's my whiskey?" the man asked.

"It's too damned early for you to be starting on that stuff," she said curtly and poured the coffee for the cowboys.

". . . And my horse backed up so fast the saddle rode up on his neck. Hell I was sittin' plumb between his ears. . . ."

"Well it's been a crazy goddamned storm. Those guys over in Sheridan really got it bad. Lost forty-five percent of their lamb crop, I heard. . ."

". . . And she went out in the morning and they was just dead cows and horses everywhere. Then her hired man come up froze to death. Christ, things is bad enough with this war going on without a mess like that. Poor woman."

Carol Lyman brought the dog's hamburger and refilled McKay's cup. "No onions."

"No onions," he replied.

One of the yardmen talked to someone behind him. "Hey, did you hear about Fred's boy and Henry? They was taken prisoner of war by them dirty Japs."

"I think I could stand anything but that," a voice behind McKay said.

"Carol, where's my whiskey at?"

"You eat that pie first."

"Well when was you hired on to be my mother?"

Carol snorted and turned on her heel. Steam from the coffee pot flew over her shoulder like a feather boa.

"Shutup everyone. . .excuse me, Ma'm. . .I think the news is coming on," one of the ranchers said.

The seat next to McKay emptied and filled up again.

"How'd you fare, McKay? Get those ornery old cows of yours loaded up?"

"Yep. I guess we did."

Carol Lyman removed the empty pie plate from in front of McKay and wiped the counter clean. Her quick movements reminded McKay of his mother. That's how his memory of her worked: nothing whole came to him, just parts of her in motion—a turbulence he could feel as she passed from room to room, a fragrance ballooning out from her.

McKay looked out the window. Someone had wiped the panes clean. The sorting pens were full again with another man's cattle and through the slats of the cars he could see the bulge of a rump and protruding horns.

"There goes more Japs," someone yelled excitedly.

A passenger train slid behind the cattle cars on another track. The shades were all drawn.

"I don't see how they could get any more in that camp."

"They say there's going to be ten thousand of them."

"Hell, I ain't even seen that many cattle in one bunch before."

Instead of the news, music came on the radio. An old cowboy with a hat shaped like a volcano and no front teeth grabbed Carol Lyman's hand and tugged at her until she came out from behind the counter. The crowd made a space for the couple in the center of the cafe and they waltzed.

McKay thought about the day his parents' car had been pulled from the canal. Something across the road had caught his eye: a woman standing in the doorway of the beauty parlor. As she watched the rescue crew, a curler dropped from her head—like an antler, McKay thought—and bounced on the floor. The woman was Carol Lyman.

"I heard Madeleine's gonna ride with them cows," the man next to McKay said.

"Yep. She sure is."

"I wonder what poor old Henry would think of that."

McKay warmed his hands around his coffee cup and said nothing.

The blacksmith took Carol Lyman's place behind the counter and started pouring coffee. He stopped in front of McKay.

"I've been thinking about your Ma and Pa this morning," he said quietly.

"Well thank you, Fred," McKay said.

"I guess you must be having a time out there...kinda lonely on that ranch, isn't it? Kinda lonely for a young man..."

McKay looked down, then out the window. His face had reddened. When Madeleine entered, every man in the cafe turned to look at her.

* * *

It was dark when the "all-aboard" sounded. Snow blew across the tall yardlights like black gravel. Madeleine boarded the train. She wore a long yellow slicker over her chaps and her hat was pulled down low against the wind.

"Call when you get to Omaha," McKay yelled up to her. "And watch for that shipping fever. I had Bobby pack the medicine kit.

And if you need help that kid from the Two Dot ranch is on board somewhere."

"Yes, McKay," she said and winked.

"And be careful. . . ."

The train lurched once and stopped. They could hear cattle scramble for footing, then the train lurched again.

"McKay, I'm sorry."

"For what?"

Madeleine shrugged. Then the train moved and she slid away from him.

* * *

McKay went to the cockfight before going home. He slid down the hill to the gravel wash under the flume. The two old men, Mañuel and Tony, were weighing their roosters on an old packer's scale. Then they dropped the birds onto the frozen ground swept clean of rock and lit uncertainly by three hissing Coleman lanterns.

The brown rooster had a speckled neck and red tail feathers. The other had black wings flecked with irridescent green. Parts of its body had been plucked and the bare skin looked blue. Bronze feathers streamed down the bird's neck. They stood on end when the birds went at each other, forming a ruffled collar.

At first the birds pecked timidly, and nuzzled neck to neck—like lovers, McKay thought. Then the brown bird jumped straight up, lashing out with his sharpened spurs as he came down. The black bird ducked, leapt and gashed back. They used their beaks and feet, pecking at each other's heads until blood came. They jumped again and when they came down this time, the brown rooster's spur stuck into the black bird's neck and blood from the jugular flowed onto the ground.

A bottle of tequila was passed. Mañuel dropped to his hands and knees over the dead rooster and when he stood again the front of his shirt was stained red. A man passed the tequila to McKay with a wild grin on his face. McKay raised the bottle in honor of the dead cock and tilted his head back until a line of stars—Orion's belt—rushed through his head. The gold liquid tasted like mineral and something overripe and very green. When they took the bottle from him he knelt down and stroked the dead rooster. "Bird of paradise," he thought, and imagined the feathers were really a woman's hair. He clutched the bird to his chest, rolled over and smiled.

McKay took the shortcut home in the dark. His horse climbed through the breaks. Snow from juniper branches spilled down his neck as he brushed by. His companion, the errant bomb, made a little wind just above his head. When the horse climbed to the top of the bench McKay could see the train, at a great distance now, shooting in a straight line east across the Basin.

He didn't know how long he rode with his eyes closed. Blasts of snow scratched his face like crushed oyster shells and the electric needle of hard cold punctured each toe. A dead rooster tied with two saddle strings, hung behind his rolled slicker. When he opened his eyes McKay knew he had reached the lower end of the ranch.

He passed the gate and climbed the knob towards the family

graveyard. When he reached the top he stepped off his horse. Snow from the ground blew up in his face, then plummeted mixing with new snow. McKay could see nothing but white. He leaned towards the ground and pawed the air: no gravestone. A noise startled the horse and the reins pulled out of McKay's numb hands.

"Shit." He kicked at snow. His foot hit something hard. He crouched down and brushed snow away but it was a rock, not his parents' headstone. Something—either the tequila or blowing snow—made his eyes close again.

McKay woke with a start and whistled. His dog came to him. He began a blindman's search for his horse. He walked back and forth, circling one way, then the other. He tripped and his hands slid across polished rock.

"Hello, Pa," he said and threw an arm around the gravestone.

"Just this once tell me where my damned horse is, will you?" he said, cupping his hands to the grave. His nose was running and tufts of blond hair stuck out from under his hat. Suddenly he stood and walked towards a tree. A dark form appeared behind the trunk.

"Well you dumb sonofabitch," he said and planted a kiss on the horse's jaw.

Snow had drifted against the tree and the horse was buried up to his shoulder. McKay began digging, working his hands the way dogs do, while the horse looked on quizzically. Blocks of snow fell away, exposing a foreleg, and shoulder, then a shuddering flank.

McKay thought about his parents, how they had been extracted from their car and pulled dead from the canal, up through a thin layer of ice that broke over his mother's head in long translucent staves; how her gray hair had come unbraided and floated like seagrass. He remembered his father's wounded, wistful eyes—how they had still been open and when he went to close them with his own hand he couldn't; how the lariat, always kept on the front seat of his parents' car in strict coils had opened across his father's chest as if to spell out one last cry of dismay: oooooooo.

Snow fell from the horse's back and knees. The whites of his eyes shone and he worked his ears. McKay grabbed the rein and led the horse from the collapsed drift. He sighed deeply, then his head fell into his blue hands and he cried.

* * *

When McKay reached the ranch no lights were on. He lit an oil lamp and wandered through the house. The snow in the living room had been mopped up—Bobby must be home. The photograph of McKay's parents had been set on the mantle over the stone fireplace and three sticks of incense were still burning.

McKay went upstairs. The old pine staircase creaked. He opened the door of the bedroom where Madeleine had slept the week before and set the lamp on a small table. For a long time he stared at the unmade bed. Then he took off all his clothes, pulled the blankets back and rubbed his aching, lonely body on the sheets where she had been.

THURSDAYS AT SNUFF'S

Suddenly I saw the cold and rook-delighting heaven
That seemed as though ice burned and was the more ice,
And thereupon imagination and heart were driven
So wild that every casual thought of that and this
Vanished and left but memories, that should be out of season
With the hot blood of youth, of love crossed long ago. . . .

—W.B. YEATS

(from "The Cold Heaven")

BRIGHT FLOODLIGHTS shone down on the mall at night, on the long dusty sheds, the front loaders, and railroad sidings. Sunrise lay pink across great mounds of tailings and left again so that by mid-morning, the mineral looked white. The mill was located at a bend in a road that came from nothing and led to nothing for a hundred miles. The only other structure was a bar across the road called Snuff's Place. Between the two, human lives were caught and suspended the way floating tree branches become snagged on sandbars. Snuff's took in and gave out people whose nervous, sour smell made the green paint peel prematurely, and the mill's pink dust blew back over the gaunt building as if to conceal its ramshackle ediface and clothe it decently.

Out back an archipelago of small cabins made a line up the hill. In the twenties, they had housed the only black madam in the state and her three employees, though after a few years they moved back to Butte, Montana, where they had come from because business there was brisker. When the Depression hit Snuff opened the cabins again, fitted the beds with worn but clean blankets and let jobless men and women coming through on freights sleep in them.

Now only one cabin was occupied. Someone called the Wildman lived there. He had fallen from a moving train just beyond the mill on a forty below zero night and when he was found, the tops of his ears had to be cut off because of frostbite. After, he stayed. At the height of the Depression he was seen acting as Snuff's chauffeur, parodying the decorous door-openings and gestures though both men wore rags.

In the one uncurtained window at the end of the bar, shaped like a porthole, a geranium plant laden with double blossoms pressed at the grimy pane. Its gnarled stalks bent over themselves, straining to soak up the autumn light. From there Snuff watched for Carol Lyman's car every Thursday. When he saw her coupé glide in under the bloodshot pulse of the bar's neon sign, he snapped on his bow tie and poured the Manhattan he had mixed for her into a stemmed cocktail glass.

Thursdays were Carol Lyman's declared "days of freedom," days on which she donned the darkest dark glasses and assumed an air of anonymity so complete she hardly knew herself. Sometimes she walked in the badlands, collecting rocks in dry washes, or when she had enough gas she'd drive to another town and drink a milkshake at a drive-in restaurant there. She thought of her ability to step out of routine as a discipline—the way some women her age do volunteer work or take up ballet.

Carol Lyman came to Wyoming in the summer of 1941 and it was already the fall of 1942 and still no one knew her well. She had arrived husbandless, with a pear-shaped retarded son and she wasn't questioned about her past. If there had been a son, certainly there had been a husband, though his whereabouts and fate were unknown.

She took part-time jobs at the shipping yard cafe and the Heart Mountain Relocation Camp and lived in a house on the very edge of the small town of Luster. The neighbors next door had a yard full of roosters who awakened her each morning. They strutted and crowed and brawled until Mañuel came out and fed them. Carol looked like a bird herself. She had long arms and legs and gnarled toes and the skin on her neck showed gooseflesh in winter. Yet she had a handsome, haughty presence, a posture that was never less than regal, and carefully kept red fingernails.

She began going to Snuff's the day the Mormon women invited her to their Relief Society Meeting. They had felt sorry for her and because wartime heightens peoples' sense of community—in direct proportion to their experience of bereavement—the women issued an invitation to the solitary Carol Lyman. She attended once. To show her gratitude she baked a banana cake and made a gallon of nonalcoholic punch, but sat back as the women made

Christmas ornaments and never joined in. During a break she went outside to have a smoke. From behind a currant bush she watched the kindly women reconvene. They kept looking up, expecting her to return. Instead she stubbed out her cigarette and drove north with her dark glasses on. That was a Thursday. She decided she would be obligated to no one from that Thursday on.

Carol drove to Snuff's on a whim. She was a guarded person who realized she had nothing to guard: her life had become as narrow as a pine needle. Snuff's bar straddled two state lines and was the loneliest place she had ever seen. That's what made her stop there.

The first time she stepped out of the car, straightened her hair, took a deep breath, and walked in. A chandelier in the center of the room swung in the draft of the opened door. Its bottom tier was bent and only four crystal prisms remained. A long cord descended through the middle of the fixture and a bare bulb hung down in the room like a punching bag. She walked to the middle of the floor and turned slowly. It was a big drafty place with a cream-colored tin ceiling blackened by soot. A sour smell moved stiffly through the air and mixed with something antiseptic. Flannel curtains with scenes of ducks and hunters pointing their shotguns hung limply over unwashed windows and the ten by ten linoleum dance floor was badly stained. There were tables and chairs and spittoons randomly arranged and at the back, a card table sparsely padded with green felt. Snuff stood between the cherrywood backbar and the marred counter where cowboys had carved their brands with pocketknives.

"You want to buy the outfit?" Snuff asked jovially, "Or do you want a drink?"

Caroly Lyman turned to him. He was tall and dapper and nearing fifty. He wore a trimmed mustache and his hair rose in a wild tuft at the top of his skull. His bright eyes danced and when he smiled his thin lips turned white.

"A Manhattan," Carol said. "Do you know how to make one?"

Snuff looked askance and went to work. He poured and shook and strained and in a moment held out the drink she had requested. She ate the cherry first, returned the stem, then drained the glass of its reddish-orange liquid.

"Very good. Thank you," she said, handed Snuff the correct change, and left the bar.

* * *

During the week, between one Thursday and the next, Carol Lyman put in time at her two jobs. Every morning she drove her son Willard to the grocery store where he swept floors and dusted canned goods. She watched as he careened down aisles with a wide broom and scattered fresh sawdust behind the polished butcher's case, while above his head cones of string spun and bounced on their spindles and were threaded down through black eyelets to the counter, then wound around white packages of meat.

It was shipping time and the cafe was crowded. Sugar and coffee had been added to the list of rationed foods and was considered one of the worst small sacrifices, though when the coffeepot emptied early in the day, no one complained. The outer ring of world misery—the Death March in Bataan, the war in North Africa, Nazi burnings and killings, the arrest of Ghandi—gyrated around local commotions: the accident in which Pinkey was hit by a car; the arrival of more Japanese Americans in guarded trains; cockfights and violent snowstorms; and the coming home of the war dead.

The next free day—Thursday—Carol drove directly to Snuff's. She had not intended to, but that's where she ended up. When Snuff saw her black coupé glide in he made a pitcher of Manhattans. Just inside the door Carol pulled a compact from her purse, primped her brittle hair, then proceeded to the bar. When she saw the drink waiting for her, she gave Snuff a hesitant, surprised smile.

"How very sweet," she said and slid onto the barstool one hip at a time.

"Hello. I'm Snuff," the tall man said.

"Carol Lyman," she said, then felt the stiffness leave her body. "It's legal to gamble in Montana, isn't it?"

"More or less."

"I'd like a card game. Is that possible?"

Snuff looked at the woman quizzically. Then he snapped on his red bow tie, for luck he said, and led her to the table at the back of the room. A pool of light lay on the green felt like a full moon. Snuff opened a new deck. His bony fingers were so long they seemed to wrap twice around the cards. He shuffled, she cut, he dealt, she asked for a card, and when she turned her hand face up he saw that she had won.

She raised the stakes for the next game and the next and won again. By mid-afternoon the pile of chips in front of her had grown tall. She looked at Snuff and started laughing self-consciously.

"I can't take all this," she said, pushing the chips back towards him, and left the bar.

* * *

During the week snow blanketed the northern part of the state, and there was a bad ground blizzard. The canary and saffron aspen leaves froze prematurely, blackened on the limb, and were blown unceremoniously to the ground. One rancher brought his steers off the mountain through the middle of town. They trampled rose bushes and vegetable gardens, ran onto one old woman's front porch, right into her living room. Then the weather turned warm.

Thursday morning Carol Lyman drove to the badlands behind her house. Wild horses ranged there in the fall and she hoped to catch a glimpse of them. She followed a road so faint it sometimes disappeared and the tops of the sagebrush scratched the underside of her car. Finally she stopped, got out, and knelt down. The white scarf she wore, a present from a man she loved twenty years before, whipped her face. In front of her were the cold hoofprints of horses. They overlapped and moved out from under her body as if running from her. The wind howled. When she looked up she saw the sky had turned violet-black—the color of a bruise. Hail fell. She pulled the scarf over her head and tied it tightly. Hail battered the back of her head and when wind shifted suddenly it beat on her face. She stood, put on her dark glasses, and drove away. Behind her the horsetracks, carved into soft soil, filled with white stones.

She arrived at Snuff's in the early afternoon. As she unwound the white scarf from her neck and head she thought it was like taking off a bandage. Her cocktail teetered on the scarred counter. The liquid swung from side to side and where it ran down the glass it left an orange residue that looked like gasoline. Snuff watched Carol drink. The dimples that showed when he smiled gave him a youthful, mischievous look. They took their usual places at the blackjack table and Carol won every game.

When the bar door swung open the chandelier swung slightly. A short man on crutches hobbled to the middle of the floor. His gray Stetson was cocked sideways on his head.

"What can I do for you, Pinkey?" Snuff asked.

"Oooooooweee. Look at all that money," he exclaimed.

"It's hers," Snuff said flatly.

Pinkey doffed his hat to Carol. One of the crutches fell from under his arm as he did so.

"I need a saw," Pinkey said.

"What in hell kind of drink is that?"

Pinkey squinted hard at the tall man. "Well you're dumber than I thought you was. What's wrong, don't you savvy English?"

Snuff grinned.

"You've got to get me outta this sonofabitch, that's what I mean," Pinkey said and kicked his broken leg into the air.

When Snuff refilled Carol's glass Pinkey peered over the rim.

"What's that hummin' bird food you're drinkin'?" he asked.

"Here, try it," she said.

"Hell no, that'd clog up my pipes."

Carol inspected the mutilated cast. It was blotched with mud and the bottom edge was badly frayed.

"How long have you had that on?" she asked.

"Too long. . . a couple of weeks, I guess."

Snuff disappeared and came back carrying a meat saw.

"What are you going to do with *that?*" Carol asked.

"Pinkey, lay back on that big table there, will you?" Snuff said. "Carol, grab his heel and kinda steady the thing."

Pinkey lay back on the long oak table, a relic from the neighboring town's one lawyer who died and whose office sat idle for twelve years. Pinkey watched as the saw sank into white plaster. Soon the cast was halved and Snuff pried it apart. They peered down at the leg.

"God it looks wormy, don't it?" Pinkey said. "Can't you put that thing back on?"

Snuff held a piece of the cast up and laughed.

"Then get me a shot of whiskey," Pinkey said.

Snuff brought the drink and Pinkey gulped it down. He slid off the table slowly until both feet, the one with the boot on and the pale one covered by a sock, touched the floor. He put weight on the broken leg, then lifted it gingerly. He tried again. Then he looked at Snuff, and at his foot.

"I'm healed. I'm healed," he cried out and waved his crutches in the air like wings. He stood up. The leg held.

"Just send me a bill, Snuff," he said and hooked the crutches on the chandelier's bent frame. They watched as he hobbled out the door.

Carol Lyman turned on her heel and gasped. The Wildman stood directly behind her. Clean-shaven, his black hair was long and matted. He had olive skin and a dappling of black moles—beauty spots—on his jaw, a dent that flattened the bridge of his nose, and penetrating eyes.

"What are you afraid of?" he asked.

In confusion, Carol looked imploringly at Snuff.

"Carol, that's the Wildman. He lives out back," Snuff said quietly.

"My dog is sick. Maybe you can help him," the Wildman said.

Carol nodded and she and Snuff followed the man to his cabin. Inside it was cramped but tidy. A narrow bed had been shoved up against one wall, a steamer trunk against another, and, leaning sideways, there was a tall bookcase crammed with a miscellany of titles: *The Virginian, War and Peace,* a set of World Book Encyclopedias, *Don Quixote,* and a stack of 1942 Saturday Evening Posts.

Carol looked at the dog. A kelpie, used for working livestock, he was smaller than a wolf but with a wolfish nose and ears.

"I found him abandoned in an irrigation ditch. He was just a little rat, a few days old. I guess they tried to drown him but someone forgot to turn the water on," the Wildman explained.

"Let's take him to the bar where he'll be warm," Snuff said.

The Wildman bundled the dog in a torn blanket and carried him to the green building. Carol had not noticed before but the afternoon was nearly gone. In the northwest dark clouds humped up and moved towards this desolate bend in the road. Despite heavy snows the week before, the air felt tropical and Carol thought she could smell the sea.

They made a soft bed for the dog under the oak table where he had always liked to sleep. He gave them a grateful, sad look. Snuff went to the porthole window and looked outside. In the distance lightning domed the dark sky with its ghostly hood of light. There was a terrible explosion of thunder overhead. Then the lights in the bar went out.

"Snuff. What's happening?"

Snuff pressed his face against the grimy porthole. Outside it was dark too: the neon light off, the mill dark, no moon. The door swung open. A small figure stood in the entry and did not move.

"Come on in," Snuff said.

Still the visitor remained motionless.

"Who's there?" Snuff asked again.

When there was no answer Snuff came out from behind the bar and fell once against the bottles.

"Snuff, goddamned it, can't you light a match or something?" Carol yelled. She heard a match being struck behind her, then another. The Wildman held up a silver candelabra.

"Where did you get a thing like that?" Carol whispered as they approached the silent figure at the door. A wizened Japanese man appeared before them. When the light shone on his face he hid his head in his hands. Then he regained his composure.

"They leave me. Cannot find way back. So confused..." he began.

"Who left you?" Snuff asked. "Are you Japanese or American?"

The old man looked at Snuff timidly but gave no answer. Snuff took the candelabra from the Wildman and went to the phone. The line was dead. He put the receiver back slowly.

"Christ," he mumbled, then rejoined the others.

A plane flew over. It made a high uneven whine that deepened into a drone as it veered away. Snuff and Carol looked up at the ceiling. Then they heard a car and two gunshots.

"What's going on around here?" Snuff said. "Maybe we better find some cover for awhile."

"Oh Snuff . . ." Carol protested, but when Snuff led the old man away from the door, Carol and the Wildman followed. Snuff helped the old man down and they all joined the sick dog under the great oak table.

"Here, give me that light," Carol said and held the candelabra up to the old man. Under coal black eyebrows he had an elfish face and a delicate upswinging nose. Gray hair was swept back from a long, grooved forehead.

"I know you," she said. "From the Camp."

"Hai. Heart Mountain. Hai," he replied cheerfully and broke into a timid smile.

"You better blow those out now," Snuff said quietly.

The Wildman held the dog close to him and in the dark they could hear the animal's labored breathing. Another plane droned overhead. This one was farther away.

"War and peace," the Wildman whispered and chuckled at his private joke.

In the confusion Carol's hand touched Snuff's under the folds of a coat he had thrown down for them and she did not move it away. They braced themselves, though for what they weren't sure—for a bomb to be dropped, for a Japanese army to burst in, for sudden death. Snuff positioned himself so he could see out the porthole at the end of the bar. Beyond the bent geranium the sky was a blank. Even the north star, the axis around which the other stars revolved, had been obscured.

Carol leaned back against the table's thick pedestal. It was like a tree, she thought, the trunk curved and smooth, and branching into a sheltering canopy. For a moment the window went white with lightning. A clap of thunder jangled the chandelier's crystal prisms. Carol imagined she was on a boat. Wind whistled and the air slipping under the door into the stale room smelled of a failing sun and seaweed.

They waited. Each tried to comfort the dog, passing him from lap to lap, stroking his hair. When the dog was passed to the old man Carol whispered. "He's just old. There's nothing to be afraid of." Then she looked at the man again. "I'm Carol Lyman," she said.

"Nakamura. Hello," the old man replied.

"Where did you relocate from?" she asked.

"Los Angeles. I was flower grower. Then had to come here. Plant garden. No good, no grow," he said forlornly.

The Wildman looked at him. "Nothing grows here except cactus, rattlesnakes and jackrabbits," he said dryly.

Mr. Nakamura gave the dog back and looked the Wildman in the eye. "Maybe he die tonight," he said.

"Yes," the Wildman said and rocked the dog tenderly in his arms.

* * *

The night was divided by long silences and short interludes of whispered talk. Snuff spoke first. He told of an upbringing in the mining town of Butte.

"I worked for Marcus Daley. He owned just about everything in Anaconda and Butte. Besides the mines he had a big hotel. It was quite a place. Everything in it was made of copper—even the toilet seats. All kinds of people came through: boxers, opera singers, movie stars, gangsters. They said Butte was an island of easy money entirely surrounded by whiskey. I was an orphan. My dad died in the mines. Oh, death was common. One man died every day in those mines; the cemetary held forty thousand. Money was easy; death was easy. I guess it was living that got to be hard.

"I grew up on Venus Alley. Do you know what that was? A whole street of whorehouses. When Mr. Daley put me to work I didn't have a dime. He taught me something about making money. I even had a little string of race horses all my own. Then I lost them in a poker game. And in exchange I got this place."

Snuff paused and looked at his surroundings, then laughed.

"I think of myself as a priest in a hardship post. I might have had a gentleman's life, but things get lost along the way," he said wearily.

Snuff's story was followed by silence. The rumbling of the Wildman's stomach broke the spell. Carol smothered a laugh, then crawled on hands and knees behind the bar. She returned with a handful of elk jerky and four pickled eggs. They were shared by all. The Wildman broke his egg in half and gave the yolk to his dog.

"What about you?" Carol asked, looking at the Wildman.

He smiled and his dark eyes bounced like wild berries stripped from a green vine.

"I fell out of a boxcar across the road. Snuff took me in."

Carol looked at him intently. "Is that *all?*"

The Wildman's eyes widened. Then he shrugged and continued.

"My ears were frostbitten. After I healed up and spring came I commenced to work as an irrigator. It's a job, like child's play. I like water. You can't hang onto it. You have to keep letting it go."

A silence followed. All eyes were on the Wildman. His matted hair sprouted straight up from his head as if he were electrified.

"Before that I was enrolled at a place called Harvard. One day I came home from class and my house had been robbed. Then I looked out at the streets and I knew why. It was the thirties, I had lots of things and other people had nothing. I wanted to know what it was like to be poor, so I rode the rails. When I returned, my parents had lost everything. I wanted to spare them the embarrassment of having an extra mouth to feed so I took off again, and landed here."

Carol's head dropped. For a moment tears stood in her eyes and dropped at an angle away from her face like a pair of dice. The small dog groaned, stretched his back legs, and collapsed again in the Wildman's lap. Snuff looked through the window. Two stars shone, then one was overtaken by clouds.

"I wonder what's happening out there," Snuff said.

The Wildman looked at him. "Nothing. The lights went out, that's all. Who would bomb this dessicated piece of real estate anyway? Did you ever think of that?"

No one answered.

"What about you, Mr. Nakamura?" Carol said.

The old man looked at her timidly. "Oh no, is no very good story."

"All stories are good," she said.

He looked from one to the other, then sat up straight and began.

"I come on ship. I'm opposite him," he said and pointed to the Wildman. "I start out with nothing. Come here to make money. Ship take long time. Very rough. People sick all over. Only one other man on board. All others—women. Picture brides. You know them? Mail order. They have photograph of man they marry. That's all. Never meet before. Just picture. Well, one woman, she so scared she jump overboard. Then her friend and I fall in love. She very beautiful. We write poems to each other every day. Like in Heian times. The day we are coming to port, we don't know what we will do. She stand in bow of ship all day looking at picture of her man. As soon as we see land, she tear it and throw to the birds. When we get off boat, there he is. Right in front. Oh, so ashamed. She grab my arm like married woman and we walk by. It is very bad thing we do but in those days, love matches not very common. Not common at all.

"After, I work for farmer. Then lease own land. Very beautiful. Right on coast, hill overlook ocean. Like Japan. We grow daisies. Many, many acres of them. So thick, I think they look like snow."

The Wildman rearranged the ailing dog and covered him with a torn blanket. Carol thought of all the places these people had lived; how they looked as if a river had run through them and swept all the small comforts away. Because it was dark in the bar, her eyes were closed sometimes, sometimes open. Maybe she would die tonight, she thought, flanked by three strange men. Yet her body felt light. She had not touched any part of a man for many years and now Snuff's arm pressed firmly against her back. A fly trapped under the dog's blanket buzzed, then stopped. The dog's eyes opened, an ear twitched, then sleep overtook him again.

"Carol?" Snuff said.

"I can't."

"Why not?"

"Because I've never told anyone."

Nakamurasan looked at her. "Nothing to lose, huh?"

Carol smiled. The Wildman relit the candelabra and their faces glowed. Carol cleared her throat.

"I spent a summer near here twenty years ago. I was young and had come to stay at a ranch. In August there was a party at a ranch on the other side of the mountain. We started out on horseback and rode all day. We arrived just as the fiddle players were tuning up. It was a lovely party. Paper lanterns had been strung across the veranda and through the trees. There were tables and tables of food. Everyone came. Even the sheepherders. I remember how they stood at the door and wouldn't come in at first. They had their dogs with them.

"During the evening I wandered down a long hall into another part of the house. I heard someone coughing, so I peeked in. A young man was lying in bed. He was the handsomest man I had ever seen. He had thick wavy hair the color of chocolate and a straight nose and big glowing eyes. Every feature was perfect. He looked like a young god lying there. He told me he had pneumonia. His cheeks were very flushed and he kept clutching my hand and asking me to stay there and talk to him. So I did. We talked about everything—there seemed to be no inhibitions. I had never talked that way to a man before. Only once did someone come in and check on him. We were alone for the rest of the night."

Carol paused, then continued.

"He was the father of Willard. I say 'was' because he died a week later. I saw it in the paper the day I was leaving to go home."

Carol looked at the others. All at once the arbitrariness of their lives seemed absurd. This bend in the road and the little towns on either side, linked by great acreages of desolation, had neither accepted nor refused them. There was room here, that was all—a geographical accident. What they had done, how far they had drifted was of no concern. The convulsions of weather and seasons would always be greater than they were. That was a comfort too, Carol thought. The bigness and strangeness of the landscape had acted on her like a drug and try as she did to reason why any of them had ended up here, she could push no clear idea into her mind.

She felt tired and cold suddenly and lay her head against Snuff's knee. A warm wind rattled the doors and windows of the bar. After awhile she slipped into a light sleep. She dreamed she was on a boat, though the seaswells she thought cradled her were Snuff's arms and the back legs of the dying dog and the Wildman's knees and Nakamura's folded hands. The boat passed over a school of fish. Then she could see herself from up in the air as though she were flying. It was not water that held the boat, but light. A clap of thunder woke her.

"What time is it?" she asked startled.

Snuff looked towards the grimy window and shrugged. Rain undulated across the darkened mill, slapped at the road and against the windowpanes, then ceased. A car drove by. There were three gunshots this time. The Wildman stood up excitedly and ran out the door, shaking the candelabra like a staff. A smell of wet sage tumbled into the room as if it had been accumulating there for years. He ran to the middle of the road and yelled: "Here I am. . . here I am. Can you see me? Shoot me. Go ahead. You can have me. Come on," he said, taunting an empty sky. As he spoke, wind extinguished the candles one by one.

Carol and Snuff went after him. A wide band of red stretched across the eastern horizon and the black began to drain from the sky. Each took an arm and led the Wildman back to the bar. Nakamura was holding the dog and singing something in Japanese. The dog's body had stiffened; he was dead.

The Wildman knelt in front of the old man and put his head to the dog's chest. After, he sat up limply. Carol put her arm around him and when he turned his head into her shoulder they could hear his muffled sobs. Carol's eyes passed over the Wildman's clotted hair and met Snuff's. They had never really looked at one another. She felt as if her body were being pressed through a screen, the soft parts flowing forward. The screen was a last restraint beyond which there were only openings.

When Snuff looked through the porthole he saw daylight. Simultaneously they got to their feet and went outside. The red belt of first light had widened: it looked like a pink shield held up to do battle with night. They sky was neither blue nor black, but pale as if the gases had been burned from it. The Wildman walked away from the others. They watched as he clambered up the pink dune of mineral tailings: over the lip of one, down the backside, up another. Nakamura pointed to the mounds.

"They are the color of fallen cherry blossoms," he said. Carol looked at the wizened old man. She thought she had never seen a morning like that, a more exquisite bend in the road. She wrapped her long arms around herself and felt ribs under her sweater. Trembling from the cold that comes just before sunrise, she rocked back and forth on her feet. Snuff looked at her.

"You look like a bride," he said.

The pink came out of the sky all at once. Now the cherry blossoms looked like drifted snow. The air took on a transparency like the hottest part of a flame. She thought she could see the stories she had heard that night skittering above the horizon, the troublesome human parts—the pain and blame—burning into the blandness of day.

A car barreled down the highway towards them. It was Pinkey and two other cowboys. They waved wildly as they passed, then the one in the back seat drew a pistol and shot three times into the air.

Perched on a pink mound, all the candles escaped from the candelabra, the Wildman started laughing. He lay on his side and rolled from the crest to the bottom of the mound and stood up at Carol's feet, his face and hair powdered thickly with dust. He did not brush himself off but walked towards the bar, his shoulders drooping slightly. As Carol, Snuff, and Nakamura followed, the neon sign over the door buzzed suddenly, lit up and began its habitual blinking once again.

1. Ursula K. Le Guin, The Visionary *and*
   Scott R. Sanders, Wonders Hidden

2. Anaïs Nin, The White Blackbird *and*
   Kanoko Okamoto, The Tale of an Old Geisha

3. James D. Houston, One Can Think About Life
   After the Fish is in the Canoe *and*
   Jeanne Wakatsuki Houston, Beyond Manzanar

4. Herbert Gold, Stories of Misbegotten Love *and*
   Don Asher, Angel on My Shoulder

5. Raymond Carver and Tess Gallagher,
   Dostoevsky (The Screenplay) *and*
   Ursula K. Le Guin, King Dog (a Screenplay)

6. Edward Hoagland, City Tales *and*
   Gretel Ehrlich, Wyoming Stories

7. Edward Abbey, Confessions of a Barbarian *and*
   Jack Curtis, Red Knife Valley

EDWARD HOAGLAND

City Tales

VOLUME VI

CAPRA PRESS
1986

For John Foley
and Joe Flaherty.

Printed in the United States of America.

Cover design by Francine Rudesill
Designed and typeset in Garamond by Jim Cook
SANTA BARBARA, CALIFORNIA

LIBRARY OF CONGRESS CATALOGING-IN-PUBLICATION DATA
Hoagland, Edward.
CITY TALES
(Capra back-to-back series)
Titles transcribed from individual title pages.
Contents: City Tales: The Witness. Kwan's Coney Island. The Final Fate of the Alligators; Wyoming Stories: Pinkey. Kai and Bobby. McKay. Thursdays at Snuff's.
1. Short stories, American. 2. American fiction—20th century.
I. Ehrlich, Gretel. Wyoming Stories. 1986. II. Title.
III. Title: Wyoming Stories. IV. Series: Capra back-to-back.
PS648.S5H6 1986 813'.54 85-25557
ISBN 0-88496-243-1 (pbk.)

PUBLISHED BY
CAPRA PRESS
Post Office Box 2068
Santa Barbara, Ca. 93120

CONTENTS

FOREWORD

The first writing I ever published was my novel Cat Man, *in 1956, when I was twenty-three. It was about the circus, and won more attention than I was to receive again for the next fifteen years. I sold a second novel, too,* The Circle Home *(1960), about the world of boxing, before turning to short stories. This is perhaps an odd way to have begun, and altogether I've published only seven stories, all of them during the 1960s interrupted by a third novel,* The Peacock's Tail *(1965)—and all before I started to write essays. I wrote more than eighty essays before returning to fiction in 1981.*

Each story, as I remember, took about three months to do, and I had a rule that once they were finished, I never let them spend a night at home. That is, if they came back from "The Atlantic Monthly" *in the morning's mail, I would send them out to* "Harper's" *that same afternoon. Most of them went to eighteen or twenty places before finding a berth. In fact, two had to have*

magazines invented for them. "Cowboys," the very first, was about a feud between some carnival men and a bunch of rodeo cowboys, and had horses in it that rather resembled the ones in Faulkner's marvelous long story "Spotted Horses." It was rejected everywhere until Saul Bellow, John Berryman, Arthur Miller, Wright Morris, Ralph Ellison and several other shining souls launched a new magazine called "The Noble Savage," *and Bellow wired me a message of Bellovian generosity:*

ADMIRE YOUR STORY COWBOYS GREATLY WOULD LIKE TO PUBLISH IT IN MAGAZINE UNDER MY EDITORSHIP NEXT SEPTEMBER AT A RATE OF FIVE CENTS PER WORD STOP. *(This was twenty-five years ago.)*

The three stories included here were written during the bachelorly, hermitic, four-year period in the latter part of that decade between my two marriages—a time when I lived in New York winter and summer and wandered the beaches of Coney Island much as Kwan does, or stared out my window at the action in front of 339 Lafayette Street near the Bowery, like the "I" in "The Witness," or imagined myself an old man with unsettling memories and a dead-end passion like Arnie Bush's, with his alligator stashed in the bathtub. In the army, like the "I" in "The Witness," I'd worked for two years in the medical laboratory at the Valley Forge Army Hospital in Pennsylvania, and had brought that experience to New York City.

"Kwan's Coney Island" was, like "Cowboys," rejected by every magazine extant, till a new one was started which would publish it—in this case, Theodore Solotaroff's "New American Review." *"The Witness," which is about as autobiographical as fiction gets,*

traveled a similarly lengthy road before George Plimpton accepted it for "The Paris Review." *"The Final Fate of the Alligators," on the other hand, struck paydirt immediately, landing in* "The New Yorker" *under the kindly aegis of Rachel MacKenzie, who fiercely and doggedly championed a series of unNew Yorkerish writers, including Bellow and Isaac Bashevis Singer, during her many years on 43rd Street.*

I found at the end of the 1960s that what I wanted to do most was to tell my own story; and by the agency of my first book of nonfiction, "Notes From the Century Before" *(1969)—which began as a diary intended only to fuel my next novel—I discovered that the easiest way to do so was by writing directly to the reader without filtering myself through the artifices of fiction. By the time another decade had passed, however, I was sick of telling my own story and went back to inventing other people's, in a novel I hope will be finished before this book you are holding comes out.*

—EDWARD HOAGLAND

Spring, 1985

THE FINAL FATE OF THE ALLIGATORS

IN SUCH A CROWDED, busy world the service each man performs is necessarily a small one. Arnie Bush's was no exception. He was living in the Chelsea district of Manhattan at this time, although he had lived in central California on several occasions, as well as Chicago and Crisfield, Maryland, and had put in four years or more in Galveston, Texas, at a point when he was married to a woman who lived there. He'd thought of it as her home rather than his; all of her husbands, as far as he knew, had left Galveston after their marriages to her ended. She owned a laundromat and barbershop, attached, which he had helped her manage. She was a cheerful, practical woman, Ellen, and they'd lived with her two sons in the cottage and patio area behind the business establishments. When he met her, he was a merchant seaman on leave from the sea, rooming in Galveston and hanging around the parks and bars, though he already knew the trade of barbering also. He'd given her a daughter, as a matter of fact—her

only daughter—whom he kept in touch with at Christmastime. The girl, whose name was Jo-ann, had grown out of her teens by now, and he was hoping she would visit him if she came North. He hadn't seen her since babyhood, but when he thought of her he imagined that she looked like her mother. Ellen was a smally built, active woman with a bumpy complexion, a pretty figure, black, scalloped hair, and masculine blue eyes. She carped and bitched a bit too much but not so much you couldn't stand it, and since she wasn't as bossy in business hours as she was at home, and since the inescapably boring chores were handled by two colored employees of long standing, he had not found that the setup interrupted his independence. Instead, he'd liked being married to a businesswoman; it furnished him with the chance to operate a going concern without the ball-and-chain aspects of owning property. He hadn't married her for money reasons, however (at least, he didn't recognize the motive if he had), but for the special, jumping, bodily impetuosity between them, never equalled for him with another woman, which really never had turned sour. Just the degree of intimacy and understanding they had reached was unforgettable; he hadn't lived four years with anyone else, or given way so much, opened himself. He'd known what she was thinking when she didn't say anything, and known that underneath the peremptory manner she was a homekeeping woman as well, who didn't want to bitch at him if she did bitch, who disliked her own bossiness and wanted peace and a simple household.

He had appreciated her youthful bottom, her mother's bosom, and the way she gathered her hair at the nape of her neck. They went to Matamoros together on a week's trip, leaving the kids

with the woman who cooked. They dressed in sombreros and paper shirts and saw a cockfight and a festival street dance, and in his memory this trip pretty well represented what a marriage ought to be like. He had delighted in the period when she was pregnant, too, partly because his own gravity had pleased him. And Ellen had slowed down—that ambitious, scrimping fussing—had leaned on him and showed a dreamy side, as he considered, like his. More than at the chance to run the business as he wanted, he'd been happy to see her soften, see her resemble him. And the whole weighty buildup to the baby's arrival—the hydraulics, the clocking of it—had seemed the marvel that it ought to be; and then the hump under the blanket and the red head and skin, the sleeping and the sucking, the rooting, the tunnelling, the reaching up, the funny-looking undershirt. He'd called her Milkmouse. He'd hung over the crib: he'd brought home cotton lambs and rubber fish, full of a welling gentleness that mixed with the detachment that was native to him and easily passed for gentleness.

There were certain moments in the routines he detested—at breakfast, for example, which they hurried through. When they were about to get up from the table, she'd mention whatever was on her mind, speaking rapidly and sharply after the silence of the meal. "I want the garbage men to clean up all that stuff they're chucking on the ground; I want you to call them about it. They can't just drive away and leave a mess like that around. And the Bendix people were supposed to be here yesterday. He knows we have two machines out. They were supposed to service us on Monday and they didn't." Sometimes she felt cornered, she said, by

the need to hammer at these guys and hold her own, making them do right, though she was thankful to have Bush taking over the worst of it. She wrangled with him at breakfast to get him started strong.

When she was with her kids, she didn't hold out areas of private reserve, but, having been somebody's wife already twice before, with Arnie she was a pensive, smiling chum at best, a speedy co-worker rather than the kind of ultimate companion he'd thought a wife would be. He resented it that what was a climax for him—his marriage—should be her third, and that she didn't flare up angrily, for instance, when a lady called her Mrs. Westrom, which was her previous husband's name. It reminded him of shacking up, or of an ordinary, carnally enlivened partnership, and he was disappointed, if this was marriage, even more than he admitted. He wasn't one to raise a stew about it, however; he was a quiet, self-contained fellow. Instead he paid more attention to the females in pearly slacks who huffed and puffed about the laundromat, eating weight-saver cookies and drinking coffee from the vending machines, and remembered the sea, of course, with intensifying nostalgia. He thought of his teens in Bakersfield and of the many memories of his twenties, when he had gone to sea and knocked around the world—afterward, he'd fought in Italy as an artilleryman. Except for Ellen, the baby, and his two stepsons, he had no ties to anyone, but he discovered that these ties were not indissoluble, either. The boys were runabouts, aged ten and twelve, not lovey or fazed at all, and Jo-ann was mostly Ellen's baby, or the cook's. Ellen's preoccupations were with the normalities of mealtimes, meeting the mortgage bills, preserving her

neighborly relationships, and seeing the children grow, whoever her husband happened to be; this was his impression anyway. She may have supposed that no husband could be held for long. She kept a bunch of photographs of herself on the coffee table and the chests of drawers to give the kids an atmosphere of family, she said. Bush, who got awfully tired of looking at them, told her she ought to go into show biz.

He was living well but was annoyed a lot. Being a believer in the rule book, a sentimentalist, he didn't like to hear her joke about their having met on the marina, as if it had been just a sort of pickup and as if she were lucky to have gotten married to the man, finally, instead of raped by him. Best were their evenings in bed, lying against the puffed pillows watching television after the kids had gone to sleep, then half an hour's succulence after lights-out, and being a person of substance the next day. He was reasonable by nature; he didn't fume and fight as his restlessness increased. But it was really not a man's life there, putting in the bluing, making change. Ellen was defeatist when they quarrelled. If she let her confusion show, he was touched; if she was apprehensive, so was he; but she was unrelenting too. In the morning, she would tell him what she wanted done in the same remote, peevish tones, her face assuming the fat expression of someone drawing on inner resources. It was as if he'd as good as left her already and she had her children and friends to fall back on. Apparently, she thought her marriages were a sort of constitutional folly. She said her friends told her she was lucky to get off so lightly every time. Who these friends were Bush didn't know; he only saw a bunch of business friends—the couple at the

bakery, the liquor man, the electrician. He didn't think her marriage to him had been foolish, but if that was her attitude what could he do?

He signed on the *Esso Chile* at last, and went off to Bahrein and Maracaibo. He was a wiper in the engine room; on other ships sometimes a steward. Actually, he wasn't on the sea for many years during this second stint before the grittiness and bleakness of the life drove him to land again; yet he did love the ocean and continued to talk about it wherever he was. In his own mind he was a seaman—a seaman ashore. He was nearly as lonely ashore and often thought of Ellen, suspecting, indeed, that leaving had been a mistake. He knew her show of indifference had not been real. She hadn't wanted him to go, but he'd let her pretend she didn't care. They'd been afraid; they'd both pretended it was a matter of small importance—he would go back into the merchant marine, she'd live just as before and maybe marry again. So the proof that he had made a mistake was that he hadn't stayed on the sea long. Every man made his share of mistakes. He missed being part of a household and painted her in pastel colors when he was disheartened, but he decided that it wasn't the mistakes that mattered so crucially as where you were at the end of them all.

Bush was doing fairly well. Stocky and aging, he had crewcut gray hair and a mustache and lived off Ninth Avenue, close to the harbor, keeping up with a few old nautical jokers who patronized the bars he went to. Like them, he hadn't seen much of the ocean from day to day, being hard at work or belowdecks in his off-hours, but what he remembered was the massive accumulation of what he'd seen. It overshadowed the other job surroundings of his

young years, just as his one marriage dominated the memories he had of other periods spent with women who for a while had supplied him with housing and with sex. He was a sailor, he told the neighbors, and at night or on his lunch hour when he took a stroll he remembered the ocean's agitated sheen, like nobbled tin, and the majestic, chastening pitch of the water when the wind blew, the ship's joints creaking, the heavily bumbering engines, the waves thudding, making a bass hiss against the hull. His apartment, although a walkup, wasn't too grim. One window faced the south, and the sunlight wasn't impeded, because the adjacent block of tenements had been torn down—a process that he knew might pose a problem for him eventually, but in the meantime his rent was low. He had a barbering position in an uptown office building, and managed to live on his salary, saving his tips.

The alligator, like an overgrown brown invalid confined to bed, lived in the big bathtub. If an outsider had been invited in to look at it, he would have gaped, because this was no ten-inch plaything but an animal of barrel-like girth, with a rakish, pitiless mouth as long as a man's forearm and a tail as long as his legs. The cut of the mouth, however, was no clue to the alligator's mood, since, like the crocodile mask that a child wears in a school play, it was vivid but never changed. The eyes, eel-gray with vertical pupils, were not as static. They seemed to have a light source within them, and the great body, scummed slightly with algae, was a battlefield shade, the shade of mud. The last time Bush had tried to determine its weight, he borrowed a slaughterhouse scale, fixed

a sling, and hung the scale from a ladder, and struggled to heft the animal into place, but he couldn't get its hind end off the ground. Even so, the scale read a hundred and thirty-some pounds. He didn't name the alligator, because it wasn't human; in no way was it human. Like Headley, the fellow who had left it with him years before, he never lit on a name that sounded appropriate—not the Trinkas and Sams that apply easily to dogs. "Alligator" did very well for nomenclature, being a title that loomed in the mind, and "you" served for talking to it.

On arrival, it had still been of a size to permit it to go through the motions of swimming, drawing its arms alongside its trunk and wriggling abruptly downward in the tub until its belly brushed the bottom and its blunt snout bumped the front. It had been four feet long then, and Headley and he had carried it up to the apartment wrapped in a blanket against the cold. The fellow, who was a barfly, a lathe operator, was going South to Gainesville, Georgia, to visit his brother and wanted Bush to take care of the creature until after the holidays. He kept saying that, as big as it had grown since he had bought it—a small water lizard in a pet store—it must be worth lots of money. But he didn't show up again.

Bush laid a plank on the toilet seat and sat in the bathroom watching his new companion porpoise and wallow for exercise as best it could. Once he realized that Headley wasn't coming back, he bought a jumbo junk bathtub from a wrecking company, paying eighty-five dollars, including the delivery charge. He could shower at work, and so the inconvenience of keeping the animal was slight. Furthermore, he soon entered into what he considered

an intimacy with it, so that he wouldn't have wanted to give it up. While he knew very well that alligators inhabit fresh water, having it in the apartment, he found a great many of his seaman's memories springing alive with a clarity even surpassing the clarity of life. The smoldering waves, the sharks and whales, the dull-colored, impassive seas on a smoky day—these sailors' sights and many more churned in the roil along with the alligator, who smelled, in fact, quite like the sea. He fed it on chunks of stew meat twice a week, not a demanding chore, and opened the window when the weather was warm to let in the sunlight direct.

At the public library, Bush read that alligators were mild-tempered compared to their crocodile relatives—that a man could swim in a slough populated with alligators without the likelihood of being attacked. He read that they preyed on waterfowl, muskrats, and slow-swimming fish, and he fed it a fryer chicken once in a while, bones included and the feathers left on. He fed it fish, too, always heedful enough in his overtures to its mouth end not to provoke an incident. The furor of feeding time was the main danger, when the alligator, after wringing a slab of meat like a rabbit, threw it up into the air for the pleasure of catching it deep in its throat when it came down, gargling the beef like a strong syrup. Splashing, galloping in place, it chomped and worried the meal, and Bush was touched because, after all, in such scanty quarters there weren't many satisfactions available to it. On less frenzied occasions, it liked to feel its throat rubbed, including the gums of its eighty teeth—just as long as he kept his hands off its muzzle, where the nostrils were, and away from its blistering, satin-gray eyes. The eyes sat on top of its head like two midget

riders, and the nostrils collapsed and blew open like a horse's nostrils when it ducked under water.

Though the books gave a vague set of criteria, he couldn't figure out the sex of his animal. He did learn that at only five years an alligator may already be sixty-six inches, which put into perspective Headley's brief role in its life; he would have been jealous to think Headley had had it longer.

Except to run water into the tub, Bush often left it to its own devices. It produced a clacking sound by chopping its teeth and at eating times it grunted, too, which he assumed was some kind of adolescent version of the drumming, reverberating boom with which full-grown alligators shook the bayous. The grunt, faintly explosive, contained an animal resonance as well—a *waw.* At the zoo, an attendant told him that alligators rarely bred in captivity, and what he observed of conditions there assured him that he wasn't unkind to keep his at home. Like an eccentric, he didn't even regard the arrangement as strange. He was a dignified man, with a serious nose, his mustache fluffy as a Russian's, and when he got a little bit drunk nobody handled him roughly. Cutting hair every day in the week but Sunday and drinking draught beer in the evening on Twenty-third Street, he had no trouble making ends meet; and he didn't acknowledge his birthdays as landmarks at all, tucking the crimping sensation of being in his sixties into his well-knit walk. He didn't resent the gator's composure, since he himself was self-sufficient.

The alligator slipped imperceptibly toward adulthood, as befitted an animal that was created to live for a century. Its corrugated back was patterned with gray diamonds, although

blurred, olive-drab colors overlaid that—not like the bright baby checks Bush saw on the specimens in the pet stores. They were yellow and black and had tiny bills, with a Donald Duck ski-jump effect at the end; their tails, though, were crenellated already and their eyes, tinted cinnamon-sulphur, were gay, iridescent, and savage.

Like a runner running a treadmill, his big friend surged in the tub, as if a birler were birling. Sometimes it inflated its lungs and then would deliberately try to submerge, swimming against its own buoyancy, until with sensuous relish it released the air and sank down. Another exercise was to seesaw, lifting and lowering its tail, making its hind legs the fulcrum—legs like afterthoughts that were tacked on. Its tail, of course, was the motive force when it swam—a walloping paddle of muscle, which the saurians of the Everglades, three times the size of his monster, swung so powerfully when they hunted at night that they could knock a drinking doe into deep water and seize her. Limber as hide, it whacked up over the edge of the tub and against the wall when the alligator wanted the sting of the blow. The tail seemed to lead a life of its own, twitching quite independently, motorized separately, and when the body moved forward, the tail, which followed after a short delay, was what lent its progress the appearance of irresistibility and crisis.

Bush provided big roasting cuts of meat now, and real mama hens. He found he was trusted more, and he could stroke the nostrils, opening and closing under his hands, or reach behind the ungainly legs to the tender, pigeon-colored armpit skin. He loved the apartment's sea smell, strong as it was, and knew that in

possessing such a remarkable prize he was erasing all of that bulk of his life when he'd stayed ashore as a dreamer, working in lumberyards and snipping people's hair.

Reptile leather in the handbag shops began to be labelled "caiman," the South American relative of the alligator. Then it was gavial skin, and the baby alligators also were unobtainable; he was told they weren't being shipped any more, though his own animal, continuing to grow, seemed prepared to live on forever on behalf of the species, linked back to the dinosaur dynasty. As its girth increased, the grin on its jaws became more theoretical, as if it were pulling the wings off a barfly in its mind's eyes, while in actuality it lived like a very fat fellow, whitening like ash gradually, its eyes a white furnace. The grin wasn't precisely gloating, however, because the two corners sliced back to the very roots of its head—there was more grin, perhaps, than the gator wanted—a grin of chagrin, a grin like that worn by a man whom events have let down and who, grinning to cover the fact, betrays the bad taste at the back of his mouth.

Bush, too, grew grizzled. He read the newspapers and kept up in a less hectored fashion by hearing the headlines read on the radio—the violent malaise of the sixties, the fads and bizarreries. There was a spate of suicides in the neighborhood, and people signalled with mirrors from their bedrooms, or blinked their lights. The streets were tight with pedestrians. He made his home his castle and used binoculars to keep in touch with his neighbors, though he was not himself overswept by the claustrophobia abroad in the world, being accustomed to shipboard conditions. He watched the

buildings smoking, and then when the city stopped them from smoking for the sake of the air, that in a way was eerie, too, because so much was going on inside you knew they ought to be smoking.

The alligator had been ill only twice, when it seemed unable to open its eyes and the eyelids turned blue. It lay with its long maw closed, and a fixed vaudeville smile, propping its head on the side of the tub so that it needn't come up for air. Bush poured bouillon into its mouth through a tube and furnished heaters, and for the time that the illness lasted he didn't attempt to exercise it. Ordinarily, hauling, assisting, he got it out onto the floor every couple of days for a walk and to let it dry thoroughly—let it lie flat, sprawling its arms, while he cleaned the interstices of its skin where fungi might gather. The logistics were not ideal, but the business was very brotherly—the struggle, shoulder to shoulder, to jimmy the heavy body out of the tub—and he didn't get tired of rubbing his hands across the rich hide. On both occasions, the alligator had got well in a week or so. There were some gradual changes, though. Whereas before when he watched the beast's clumsy galumphing he had imagined the alligators in the swamps in their glory, now he began to see his friend just trying to stay alive. The alligator stared at him through its imprisoning mask, a pleasure-pain mask, although its cruel pupils contained all the harshness of millenniums past—and he wasn't so sure it was going to outlive him. A man downstairs kept fish, and Bush arranged that if he should die this person would telephone the zoo and get them to take the alligator safely. Since *he* wasn't made to last for a century, he hadn't expected that he might outlive his friend.

Besides the problems of fresh air and space, there was the elaborate question of diet. How could he duplicate the crunchy, glittery nutrients of a jungle river? Of course finally he couldn't—not with powdered Vitamin D and not with steer beef. Sometimes the alligator loped like an otter with constipation, humped awkwardly, and when that happened his own belly ached. These seizures disturbed him dreadfully, especially when he decided they were the result of a deficiency, and one he couldn't correct. Dancing like a bear that had burned its feet, the creature suffered sadly, though its mask was still heavy and comic and rigid. Great gouts of gas came up in bubbles, released from the alligator's digestive tract after much lurching and shuffling. It craned its neck to persuade them to come, after doing an agonized gandy dance, or a dance of death.

During the night one weekend, at last, it died. Bush didn't discover the fact until midmorning, because its position underwater was painless-looking and natural, the head floating just in the attitude of an alligator at peace with itself; he only noticed that it was dead when he saw that it didn't come up to breathe. However, the expression was a terrible one. The expression was like the Angel of Death's, if, as seemed likely, an alligator confronts the Angel of Death with the expression of the Angel of Death. And all of those aeons were etched on the mask—all of the meals in the bubbling mud, the procession of species extinguished, the mountain-building, the flooding seas and the baking sun. The framework of daily courtesies was over between them, and the fury and barbarism photographed on the face were alive like a flame.

He might have called in the leather-toolers, but didn't. He and his neighbor who kept fish got help and carried the alligator down to the street late Sunday night, leaving it stretched in solitary magnificence across the sidewalk for the city to figure out what to do with.

He had these three memories, then: the sea, the few years in Texas, and the years on Twenty-first Street, with the mumbo-jumbo that filled in between.

KWAN'S CONEY ISLAND

THERE WAS A SAINT in the streets, a bland silver man about one-fourth-sized who was rolling along on a rubber-wheeled cart while a priest in lace walked in front reading the blessing. Two lines of men gently pulled the lead ropes and behind the saint's cart a large number of women in black carried candles. A uniformed band of fifteen played a salute to anybody who came up with a dollar bill to be pinned to the saint's vestments. "Wait a minute! Wait a minute. Not so fast," said a butcher coming out of his store after the crowd had gone by. He wore a black band on his arm and, holding his dollar, he kept at a sensible step to catch up with them. The band turned, like everyone else, to wait and, when he'd delivered it, did the salute, all the cheeks puffed, the instruments facing him. He got a saint's card from the priest which his wife kissed.

Kwan nodded familiarly to the marchers. These parades happened almost every month. He followed until the fireworks

stage, when a string of firecrackers were laid down for a block and the head man waved his breast-pocket handkerchief a long time, swearing because his assistants at the opposite end couldn't figure out what he meant. Then a shocking great war cannonade went off, filling the air with its smell and smoke. The kids ran the length of the fuse just ahead of the blasts, and yellow and blue and red stains were left in the street which would last till the next occasion. The saint was rolled into a storefront to stay.

Kwan had been downtown for Saturday night and had come back late on the bus. This morning, delightfully logy, he'd lain in bed past eleven o'clock, although he was never a sound sleeper. He lived in the back of his laundry, not to save money so much as because he had gotten to be rather crusty and could do without constant company. He liked company only in short doses. After a get-together he took at least a couple of days to digest whatever he'd heard and several more days to finish enjoying it. He had lived in Pittsburgh for many years, so to live here in New York a few dozen blocks from the central neighborhood of his own people was a luxury. In his block were black men and Puerto Ricans and Sons of Adam, as he called the Hasidic Jews, and Italians, as he called the Germans, Poles, Greeks, and Italians, and miscellaneous bums and bearded young scholars. He had a Russian church and a Spanish church alongside his business and, all in all, he could pass in and out with a fine anonymity. Sundays in August now he went to the beach, thinking over the gossip of Saturday night and the fixes his friends had gotten themselves into. Even on a cool day he would go because of the sweltering week he'd put in, as well as the sweltering week to come. He was

middle-aged, dressed in his next-to-best suit and a clovered sport shirt, with the mild roundish face of a member of the amphibia family, except for his humorous mouth and firm chin.

The hydrants were going but nobody soaked him as he went past; the Puerto Ricans were after their own. It was a day in the eighties with a marvelous high sky the blue of an organdy robe. He took the subway, reading a Chinese newspaper until the tracks emerged above ground. Having chosen his seat especially, he sat back, his hands clasped in his lap, blinking in the sun, and fanned by a dry city breeze. Although his appearance was staid, he was just as pleased at the holiday as the children who chased back and forth in the car. They were more than pleased—they jumped on the seats, they shoved each other against other passengers and part way out of the window. The train made a great many lackadaisical stops, while Kwan mused down at the street below. At Coney Island the pour of humankind off the platform and the festival babble and crush got him energetic. There were mynah birds telling fortunes, merry-go-rounds making music, coin-slotted player pianos. On the hurtling rollercoaster, people screamed and screamed. From the pots at Korn's Korn came a scarifying smell like flesh burning, and the teen-agers, running in front of the traffic, plunged for the beach. It was all too much, of course, and reminded him of scenes from his boyhood in China, but he was detached and quick on his feet, inconspicuous, knew what he liked, and liked this contrast with the rest of the week.

He went to his bathhouse establishment. STEAM, the signs said. A lot of the men spent the whole day reading the newspaper in their cubicles. They sunned for a bit on the roof, steamed in the

steam room, and never went out on the beach. Kwan sampled the services, getting his money's worth. The fat stomachs on the Italians amused him. Though he was certainly no muscle-man, they were so laughably fat that as soon as they took off their belts they had to hold onto their bellies. Their testicles bulged like bunches of onions. To squeeze in for a shower was like having to push through a herd of beach balls. It was always quarrelsome, because most of them weren't alone through the week like he was but were standing up for their rights in some busy business establishment, and they couldn't lay off on Sunday. And the black-white business was tense. Only a handful of blacks came in to change, but today one of them attached on to Kwan to try to get into the showers. He was in the next cubicle and he offered Kwan part of a sandwich, struck up a conversation until Kwan left with his towel, and then hurried to swallow and stand up too, more and more nervous about it.

"It's pretty packed, huh?"

"Plenty room," Kwan assured him.

The trouble was that his fear was contagious; for a moment Kwan was afraid to go into that bald gleaming mass of bodies himself, forgetting that nobody ever objected to him. The black hardly looked at him, he was so busy being nonchalant and looking ahead to the white men's faces.

"Any space?"

Kwan paused beside the Negro, but there were so many people talking that nobody answered. He pushed through to find a spot, the man tagging after, putting a shoulder in Kwan's stream of water and sloshing his front with one hand. It was a crazy room,

with shapes such as you never saw on the street, and much genital-fussing and belly-rubbing.

The exit to the beach went under the boardwalk, where the whites were the jittery ones. The shade was dazzlingly striped with thin lines of sun and a good crowd of people had sprawled in the cool twilit sand. Mothers held kids. The passive families with their spraddled-out postures and scraps of food reminded Kwan of a refugee crowd, and the stripes across everything were doubly weird, but the sea glittered peacefully blue. He had on a new bathing suit and his toes had not grown as old or as crooked as some of these fellows' toes. Adding it up, he cut not a bad figure, he thought. Nobody took exception to him.

A bunch of colored children tore by, throwing handfuls of sand. There were drunks with beer cans, tough policemen, and propped, melancholy souls alone on the part of the beach where everyone else was in transit. They lay on one elbow with their lonely detective novel and their plaid thermos bottle and their brown fleabag blanket from home. It was stop-go. A pair of whites would find themselves on a collision course with three blacks and suddenly stop. By the water the hot sand got cold. Jammed family groups whooped it; screwballs were yelling. The continual verging on violence was tiresome but didn't directly affect Kwan, who picked his way out beside one of the breakwaters until his body was lapped by the waves. Facing the sun, he braced his back against a large rock and dug his heels in, loving the suctioning. This was his favorite time of the week, right now. He wiggled around for the perfect position, worried that soon the day would be gone, that he wasn't happy enough, but he was. The light,

multiplied on the water, was a week's worth of sun. He had seaweed to scrub with and salt on his lips. He smiled so much that he wasn't aware he was smiling, and was all the time closing his eyes to enjoy them closed and then opening them to watch the shimmer and action. Probably five thousand kids were being taught how to swim just in the area in front of him, which made for a steady myriad blare, the yeows and shrieks yipping out of it. Jumping, jumping, jumping, jumping—there was scarcely space for the waves to roll in. When the wind cut the hooting, it blew back again. Old-man-in-the-moon faces bobbed up to blow out the water and suck in some air. Horses chased horses. Mothers were teaching by every method, including the drown-'em-and-laugh-at-'em-cry, if only because they themselves were scared. The lifeguards paddled on little rafts which the fishy kids tried to catch up with, and once they had a shark scare, when the police helicopter started to swoop. A guy clambered out covered with black steamship oil, having swum through a slick. He'd been the shark. In the distance the regular skyride screams were like crying dolls squeezed.

Five children crept past after crabs, although the rocks had been hunted clean. Kwan tried to converse with them with avuncular dignity, pretending to peer round his feet in case a crab might be hiding there. He liked their shouts and the teeming water and teeming beach, the women in bouncing bathing suits. While he regretted not having had children, this was not a gnawing or painful feeling because it had never seemed possible. Marriage had never been much of a hope. He'd paid court to several ladies but always as one of so many suitors that the family

and daughter had toyed with him, letting him know how privileged he was. Even so, he had various dear memories of the onanist's kind—vigils outdoors, or missing a meal to send flowers he knew that the girl would ignore. Sometimes he'd encountered a colored woman who would come in the back and allow him to tickle her a little instead of charging her for her laundry, and then he had hoped that a permanent amicability might grow up between them. But each time afterwards when he mulled it over, he realized it would only amount to a lot of tickling—no work. If he wanted to share his life with someone, he needed a helper. The flight to Hong Kong to bring back a wife required an enormous sum. To be sure, he had saved toward it, but he was an occasional gambler and he loved his other few pleasures too much.

The mobs were a piece of his childhood, the kids smeared with black sand. He strolled way down to the fishing pier and sat against a green piling. He saw an eel caught and a beer-bottle fight between the men on the pier and the men in the motor boats which were putting about, tangling some of the lines. There was a fight on the beach as well. The white lifeguards in the towers close by had to jump down and help one of their bunch against ten or twelve Puerto Ricans. The police got into it with roaring and clubs and the kids on the sidelines grabbed several girls by the heels and dragged them around, scaring them into hysterics. It was serious for an instant; then it fragmented. The unearthly hordes of people, picnicking, petting, quietly wading, swallowed everything up.

With sharp interest, Kwan watched the ocean-going ships rendezvous with the pilot boat at the mouth of the Narrows. As a

boy he had wanted to go to sea and still thought of himself as half seaman, especially because of his one long sea journey. At night in his shop he listened for toots from the harbor, sniffing the salt smells. He liked to walk, so he walked some more, keeping a count of the ships he saw and prolonging the afternoon's activity. When people spat near his feet on the sand he spat back, if not near enough to set off a brawl. The beach was extremely hot. He got up on his toes and trotted under the boardwalk again with the shade-loving crew. The Seashell Bar was there, a whole line of bars, and this was his day for American food. He leaned on the counter as sauerkraut was forked on his sausage—"Very good stuff. More, man." With big Chinese mouthfuls he ate a whole lot. A raving white man kept pulling his trousers off, while the cops attempted to tie them up during the wait for the ambulance. Finally they needed to handcuff him in order to keep them on. He shrieked like a factory whistle and collected a crowd. Kwan scraped with his teeth at a candied apple and winced at the smell of the cooking corn.

The sea was a sizzling, glistening blue. He watched the Parachute Jump, the kids doing stunts. He watched the Diving Bell sink down in its tank where it was nosed by the Porpoise Herd. Couples being jolted out of the funhouse doors at the end of their ride were bloated by mirrors to squeal a last squeal. At the Torture House an elephant was mashing a canvas man underfoot. Santa Claus laughs came up from him. The sign "Chinese Water Torture" intrigued Kwan, since he couldn't guess what that might be. Finally he paid the twenty-five cents. The House was a tent behind a board facade, and the Water Torture was not featured

prominently. Both victim and tormentor were yellow as bile, the latter chuckling, apparently. The victim looked up with the face of a calf about to feed, head twisted around to catch hold of the teat. He was papier mâché, and a make-believe faucet dripped on him. Quite accurate characters in a pencilled balloon said, "Let me go." Kwan grinned at all this, but some of the other exhibits made him squint; he had squint lines engraved almost like a sun-squint.

There was a live show. A fat man climbed slowly onto the stage. "Folks can come right down close to me where you can see everything and hear everything. No need to be afraid of me. . . ." His face was tattooed as if he'd wished to obliterate it, not simply to become a rarer freak. He had a display case of hatpins and needles and two rows of drinking glasses.

"All you good people want to see everything, want to hear everything. That's what you have here, all the odd people," he said, filling the glasses to different levels, and continued in a mesmerizing, biting voice, "My name is Musical Tons." He laughed to get his body shaking, groaning at the discomfort. "I'm fat, but since I'm not as fat as some I'm also musical." He licked his finger and began to rub the glasses' rims. He did "Dixie" and "I Could Have Danced All Night." But the audience grew sarcastic and whistled along. "Mary, to my right, is one of our features. She's going to talk to you about herself in her own words and will glad to answer any of your questions. Please listen carefully."

"Now you were told outside on the paper that I would show you underneath my dress, and that's what you are seeing," said Mary, who was unbuttoning her dress in mannish haste. The people giggled with whispers. Faint howls drifted from the

rollercoaster. She wore a bathing suit. "I am a Christian woman and I do not show you underneath my bathing suit. It is the same. The ladies may feel of anywhere they wish to be convinced that it is real. The gentlemen may feel of anywhere where they would feel their sisters or their mothers. Now I have cards for ten cents which show myself and I will write on them my name Mary in my own handwriting, which is very good."

She spoke fast and she wrapped the dress around her like a towel.

"Now I am called the Crocodile Woman, which is because my skin is like the thick skin or the hide of a crocodile. It is because of a disease, and which is not infectious, do not worry. I am a Christian woman the same as your wife or your mother. Now I have a message for you, which is that God loves you. Enjoy the life which God has given to you, enjoy your skin, be thankful."

"Thank you, Mary," Musical Tons said into the microphone. "May I direct our friends back to myself? I am going to perform what has been called in the newsprint a remarkable demonstration of hardihood. Pay close attention, if you please."

He took his shirt off. There were hooks through his nipples, and he picked up two five-pound weights from the floor with them. "I'd do the heavier ones if we had a bigger crowd." He smiled around. He had separate smiles for the whites and the blacks but in both cases bitter with scorn. As he swung into doing his stuff, what politeness he'd had before peeled away; he was intense.

"What I do mostly is stick these pins through myself. Want me to?"

"Yeah," called the crowd, caustic and mostly young. He grinned at them and they back at him. The Santa Claus *ho*'s came from the man being mashed by the elephant outside, and Kwan's squint was well-rooted by now, not much more distressed than a standard sun-squint but limiting the amount that the eyes took in.

"You do?" Turning a bit toward the knot of whites, he dawdled, as if such a personal stunt was humiliating to perform in front of a bunch of Negroes, who were quick to sense this, however. Several pressed in, looking at all those blue bruises.

"Which arm?" he asked.

"Lef'!" they shouted. And plenty of whites were panting as well, until his contempt grew so delicious to him he couldn't bear it and wheeled around to the blacks again.

"How about both arms?"

People broke into smiles and nodded. He leaned from the stage, stroking the longest hatpins. "You may expect I sterilize these things. No, as a matter of fact, just the opposite." He dropped them and rolled them under his shoe. "The trouble is, a platform like this is never awfully dirty; not the real vicious germs. How about it? Put some on for me, would you! Give me some germs."

Ha! They were startled. Those who didn't freeze up were excited. "You want to get poorly, huh? Over here, babe!"

Musical Tons mixed his colors and took from the young and the old, leaning out to give everybody a chance to contribute the smudge off their hands. The women acted as if they were touching a snake, and one fellow had a real brainstorm and licked the pin when it came to him.

"Good. Let's get the worst of it. Give me some more."

He picked a white volunteer to help push the needles through. "You're not much use, are you? Is he, folks?" It was hard going with the first one, particularly on the far side of his arm. The point was dulled so that nothing important inside would be cut. Once the pain started, though, his zest went away; he was deadpan. It seemed like distasteful labor to him rather than pain. Kwan felt twinges penetrating his limbs too.

Anguished figures around the room were painted with blood, but he might have been digging a sewer hole. When he had hatpins sticking through both his arms, "How's this?" he said. "Enough, or do you want'em through my legs too?"

"Up your old ass, man. Let's see the whole thing!"

He smiled toothily like a dog. "Everywhere? Okay, but your job's the filth. I want all you have. Armpits, that's right, you got the idea."

The racial divisions were gone. It was between those who froze and those who warmed. The pins that were already in obstructed his muscles when he was pushing the new pins through and he looked like a man from Mars equipped for space signals. "How about it?" He pointed to marks on the side of his neck. "Sometimes if I have a big crowd I'll put one through here. Are you people big?"

"Yeah, big. Big as butter," they yelled, with the grins of a gangster movie emptying.

He laughed. "No, you're not. You're too small." He drew out the pins and rubbed the blood drops at each exit point into one of his hands like a powder.

* * *

Kwan loafed in a bingo parlor for an hour—a collection of souls who were more his own age. The sun got low. The whistle-pitched roar from the beach subsided. Instead there were drumming parties and bonfires, shouting and stone-throwing. A girl belly-danced. Gangs of kids with handkerchiefs around their heads were swinging clubs. The beach was like a checkerboard, with whites in certain parts and blacks in other parts. Kwan watched the pitching machines pitch baseballs and watched the Scorpion, the Steeplechase. The lights strung over all of the rides went on, and a boy ran along the boardwalk setting the wastebaskets afire. Kwan steamed in his bathhouse again. He sat in a bar, played bingo another half-hour, then saw the jail pen cleared. As this was underneath the boardwalk, an amphitheater was formed around it by the ramps going up. A large crowd gathered, and, since the prisoners came out singly to the paddywagon, the process was a long one, each fellow making his moment in the limelight just as dramatic as he could. For some it was the last steps of a death march, for some the last steps to the stake. They stalked like concentration camp victims. They wept dementedly and stumbled, protesting, with glances at the sky. Soon afterward the riot that had been brewing finally broke out. It wasn't anything to see, just cobra-mongoose-jumping and strangled yells, figures running dimly and hammering down with their sticks. First the Italians were outnumbered and then the blacks. New blacks came, more Italians, and then again new blacks, who were sweeping the beach when the cops sirened in.

Kwan wandered through a side alley to get a last feel of the sand. He took his shoes off for the fifth time today. He couldn't decide whether to go straight home or stop downtown along the way.

He noticed a colored woman who was sitting against a post in the darkness near him. "Hey you," she said. He was cautious—he had started to leave—but turned and edged toward her, kicking ice cream cups and paper plates.

"I'm Chinese," he said.

"I know you're Chinese. Nobody's mad at you. Nobody's going to beat you up." She laughed. The feet on the boardwalk sounded over them.

Lying down, he put his hands behind his head and clasped the post. She fixed a piece of cardboard in the position of a lean-to. Although she was only a youngster, she had a face with glamorous, rich lines, a nose that flared out when she smiled, and very pretty creases in her forehead with which she could pretend surprise.

"I'm Crystal."

He was impatient now. In his old boardinghouse a Cuban girl had tapped along the rows of single rooms each night, being quick and businesslike.

But she insisted. "Say it."

"Clystal."

"C*ry*stal!" she giggled. "No, C*ry*stal. Say it."

"Clystal." He clutched the pole and watched her tongue.

"C*ry*stal. You trying?"

"I hold on," Kwan said.

"Yes, you hold on as hard as you can. First say it, though."

"Clystal."

"C*ry*stal!" she shrieked in giggles, making him wait.

THE WITNESS

I HAD BEEN TRAINED as a hospital technician in the army, and instead of the gleaming lab job uptown by which I had hoped to pay for graduate school, I was working in a defunct office building on the edge of the Lower East Side. It was a lab job, but what a lab! My cornflakes-and-cream face began to thin. I lived in a hair-raising rooming house, wondering what my BA was going to be worth and what would become of me. At the same time, however, life down there seemed bracingly rich. The pigeons of Venice wheeled over the roofs and the fountains of Rome spouted up from the hydrants. Churches in eight languages. You could buy diamondback terrapins and whole sheepskins, octopuses and sackfuls of beans. I still think somebody who lived near me could have traveled all over the world without seeing a face which really surprised him. The streets had the spicing of danger a young man likes—"Count Draculer" ruled in the block. Next door to my room was a death's-head guy who wept more than most people laugh.

"My wife, my poor wife." I used to smile when we met on the stairs, being polite and supposing that he was laughing, until finally I distinguished the words. The family across the backyard kept roosters which woke me up in the morning.

Where I worked was a bleaker, Chicago-like district of factories, empty at night. It had been bustly about 1900 and was full of April-fool structures with gargoyles that goggled down. A fop stood on the edge of the roof of a perfume warehouse looking into an oval mirror. A large Christ close to him held a cross, and our wild-faced, collapsing building had MARY along its front in archaic lettering between wreaths of stone. My boss was a man named Darwin Hanes, forty-five. He wore a Purple Heart pin, and ties that announced that he was probably a fruit. He was earnest, kind-natured, a flurrier at work, and rather the pure scientist in his intentions, except that he'd flunked out of medical school and dieted on nothing but personal bloody noses in the twenty years since. Anyway, he kept a room for projects of his own, with tubes of Tb and guinea pigs sneezing—we mopped down the floor with iodine. He was round-faced, pouch-eyed, and he made his acquaintances uncomfortable by staring at them for long, long stretches when he talked to them. Alone in the world, he was in that state seen commonly in New York where you give the person about five more years before he goes into a mental ward.

His cronies were Puerto Ricans, flattered to have an American friend. Darwin had learned Spanish during one of his self-improvement spates, and blew hot and cold on them, both sexually and just as chums. Hot and cold otherwise, he was touching answering the phone, full of belief and civilization and a

scientist's pride; then the choked pain in his voice (the doctors thought him a nut) when the man on the other end said he was sending a couple of patients over for tests and expected a kickback. He'd start shivering slightly, almost as though exhilarated. The world was all black, and, bastard of bastards, he'd make his way! If the girl in question came in with starched sleeves she preferred not to roll up for her blood test but took off the blouse instead, Darwin insisted on coughing until, despite my embarrassment, I pushed in to watch. He had a blackboard on which he did gene transposition equations, patterning himself on J. Robert Oppenheimer, perhaps. He'd put on a mystical stare and brush at the chalk on his hands absently, living the life of a genius as far as he could. He would come in in the morning having "seen the whole thing in front of me" just before falling to sleep, and would sit half the day at his desk muttering over the records he made of experiments, without much result—he'd "lost it."

A great man's life was variety, so he never stinted on phone calls or shopping around for equipment. He was interested in immense centrifuges, in the newest of sterilizers, and barrels of culture media. He believed busy men picked up the phone on the first ring—"Yes, yes, this is he"—taking notes on the margins of whatever was close. He had a soft voice that strung the salesmen along.

There wasn't much work, although enough not to pass the day reading, and I looked out on Lafayette Street a good deal, which was a large brutal one-way thoroughfare, always a drama in progress. At my window I got to be sort of a fixture. The drivers sped by, keeping up with the lights, and under the traffic's roar it

was hard to distinguish other sounds, only the most frantic yells. More than once, happening to glance outside, I noticed everybody on the street had stopped and faced in our direction because of some appalling thing which had been going on underneath us for several minutes. A cross-section of business people came into the area, along with the garment workers, but the neighborhood acquired its peculiar tone from the bums wandering in from the Bowery a few blocks away. Though they were only a handful at a time, because of them nobody could ask for a drink of water at the soda fountain, get a car pushed, or ask any favor whatsoever. When the traffic light went kerflooey we must have had six or eight accidents before it was fixed, since everybody assumed someone else had called up about it. They were shoeless and bloodied bums, heaving, gasping and threshing bums. One never knew what might be wrong with them and never investigated. Once during the summer I remember a woman sat on the sidewalk from lunchtime on, apparently making different sounds. Several men stopped and peeked up her skirts but didn't do anything for her. A telephone company driver talked with her awhile from his truck; and a lady and a friend did busy themselves, except that they hurried on all the more hastily for their distress when three cabs refused to carry the woman anywhere.

It wasn't possible not to watch, just as it wasn't possible for me to be very effective in helping without that becoming a full-time job. No one else did any more, not the priests or the nuns walking through, not the cops, though the cops did whatever eventually was done. The station house soon knew my voice as a crank's. It seemed I was running downstairs all the time—feeling pulses,

dragging bums who passed out out of the road. I considered myself a kind of a last resort. The gas station group across from us would boot a man in the seat of the pants and bait him into "insulting" them so that they could grab their billy clubs, wrenches and tire tools and give him the run of his life. I shouted as loud as I could; I'd point from my window, establishing that I was witnessing it. Darwin never looked out, even when nothing was happening, and if he saw me hunch up from what I was watching, he left the room in a blaze of exasperation with the street and with savagery and with his own tender heart. He was sometimes hysterically harsh when he found a derelict trying to get warm in the hall but then was unhappy the rest of the day.

I was the laughing, skinny young man full of "minority" sympathy. I'd laughed at fraternity life, laughed at the army, and now in uncertainty I laughed at the city here, although it was the thinnest defense. In the bazaar-like streets around where I lived I began to flinch at the richness, not that it didn't delight me but because I was living amidst it too; nobody was going to come get me out. I had a girlfriend in the building named Ida with a pre-school son and a husband long gone. We shopped from exotic market stalls or ate in great Chinese restaurants or went to the Statue of Liberty. She had nice black hair when she looked after it but malnourished skin—an eager vulnerable girl scalded as tough as a cat. Her eyes were marvelously brown and big, a very light, shining brown. We used to joke that she polished them, and, without contradicting the skepticism which had got knocked into them, they fluttered with accessibility. The lids constantly closed as if holding them in when I turned on my little charm, such as it

was. Since she was the first person who'd ever been specially taken with it, I turned it on as hard as I could.

How she needed a man. She'd trot at my heels as close as a colt when we went down the stairs. She was a Japanese whorehouse in bed, and scornfully mocked me for being a mere boy, years younger than her, when her lopsided liking for me stuck out. She ate on eighty-five cents a day Welfare money with Tony, her son—powdered milk, pork hearts in government cans, and peanut butter. She fried powdered eggs and baked surplus flour. Forkfuls of butter and peas were a pleasure to her, and herring on crackers or a lamb chop was food for a queen. Her boy needed galoshes and toys and everything else and already worried about his mother. "Somebody" would give her a new pair of shoes, "somebody" would give her a sweater, he said, much too young to be hinting. He'd ask me to carry their garbage can down, and if I had change from an errand I'd done for Ida, he ran to her with it as if it were some kind of medicine.

She got colitis, bladder infections, aches in her ears, and every few days appeared to be out of her mind—she yelled in a hollow monotone. Her ovaries formed knots from nervous tension, and it was at one of these times that she thought she had gotten pregnant, which pulled us apart even as we pretended to join together. Fiendishly helpless, she was dependent on clinic interns and procedures whenever she or Tony got sick, and since the furnace broke down about once a week, this was often. At midnight Tony would suddenly wake up laboring to breathe, his temperature a hundred and two. A doctor or ambulance wouldn't be sent unless it went higher than that; and without my handouts

she hadn't a cent for a taxi. One autumn night when I wasn't home she went into the street with him in convulsions in her arms, and found and convinced a patrolman that help should be called, afterwards standing beside him for twenty minutes. He was a young man and kept wanting to stop the police cars which passed. He went up on his toes, looking to see if the policemen were friends, but knew he would only be reprimanded for not having waited for the ambulence. In all these problems, the money I gave her was scarcely a starter because if her sanity really had cracked for as long as a couple of days, wheels would have been set into motion by the Welfare Department for taking her son away.

With each of us frightened, we sometimes had quite ecstatic excursions, as gay as one gets when the roof may fall in. We rolled the stroller along the East River at Delancey Street. The freighters that came sliding by seemed to fill it completely. We'd race them, while Tony hollered. I was fascinated by him. Week by week he was developing, and very much looking around for an older male. He watched me shave in the morning—"Is that how we do it?" He peered in when I took a shower and came up for regular battles with me. I grew very tender, toting him upstairs when Ida stayed late in my room and we put him to sleep on my couch. Then they spent the night, both in the bed. Such cooking, and dashing with tidbits for me—if she didn't claw me she gave me the moon. Once I had become a passion, she used every tool. She encouraged my fondness for Tony and told me he loved me, prompting trips up by him too to say that he did. The next time we were alone, he would say carefully, "I don't love you, Gene. I

don't, you know." She thought me elegant, gentle and fine, and the security she needed so desperately came into it.

We went out at five in the afternoon, when the pigeon-fanciers were up on their roofs. White swoops and black shadow patterns. And every Friday a farmer sold tomatoes, comb honey, and cider and cheese in the storefront he rented—yellow cream, to make the sick well, and even cornflowers in the summer. He talked Ukrainian with his old neighbors, having left Ninth Street twenty-five years before. It was a link for him, and he was the man who'd made good in their block, and their tie to the woods and fields. He had flat farmer's arms, blue eyes, and a reprobate's face, the slack cheeks and lax mouth. "Just the pure stuff, nothing put in it," he said, like an article of faith, when we asked if the cider was sweet. His pear crates and his heavy old shirt and work boots were as good as a trip out of town.

Often we whooped out to Tompkins Park where there were the modern, sinuous slides. Dusk was the ideal time. Tony crawled through the whale-shaped pipes, giving out screams, and went up to the other children. He always seemed infinitely dearer than them. I followed as if he were mine. He'd negotiate some over a toy, then turn to me and throw his ball, or hike onto a higher slide, wheeing down with the tentative relish of someone enjoying what he knows is likely to be his chief recreation for the day. He always was interested to hear what we thought he'd particularly like to do next year, and he enjoyed these dusk go-rounds in much the same way that we did, for the magical sinking light and the teeming park emptied except for a few muted kids at the swings. He climbed the big slide with boosts from me—it was too high for

him—and slid cautiously down. One afternoon they all had got hold of a pup tent and we helped put it up on the baseball field.

Tony had a luminousness, a resonance to him that was pitched very clear, a sing to his affections and words, perhaps just from growing up in a kind of state of emergency. After each bout with flu he seemed changed, a little bit older. He had awful dreams and toilet troubles and slept with his mother, but otherwise wasn't more nervous than plenty of children, so that whatever effect all of this would have was left in the air. Though he cried during Ida's lengthiest rages and spent many consecutive hours at the TV with that deadweight stare of a child, he remained promising. Of course Ida's hope was Tony in school, that here he would get the support he needed; some bright, cultivated teacher might take him in hand. He'd begun at a pilot-program nursery school and the teachers excited her with their comments. She and I had our ups and downs. My helping hand would be abruptly withdrawn, if only because she'd refuse it. In a day the world of dried Navy beans would return, the hard-as-nails mother. There was a lesbian middle-aged woman who paid Ida's phone bill and gave other aid in emergencies in exchange for the loan of the place certain mornings, and these visits increased. The plastering fell more frequently, provoking wilder reactions. The laundry piled up when the hot water failed and fifty cents wasn't forthcoming from me to take it around the corner. I wouldn't know what was happening downstairs, except that I'd hear a groan or two when I went past and resolve all the more to keep my distance, tired of catching sore throats from them, but worrying about the boy.

That Christmas: what a Christmas that was. No money, his

mother bewailing into the phone. She'd determined to find some means of buying him a decent spread of presents but she had failed, and the failure knocked all her palisades down, the wolves howled—she was terrified about everything. We had had no contact for a couple of weeks, but the day before Christmas I overheard part of it and went down with a ten dollar bill for a tree and so forth.

"For who?"

"For Tony and us," I said, in the door.

"More games. More games and games and games," she told me in the most utterly exhausted tone, although already letting me rub her forehead. She rocked with it. "The dog act," she called it.

"You won't leave me alone. You won't stop knocking, will you? I must fill a function for you. I'm a pool you can splash in and see some results. You can see what a kick you have. You won't stop dropping in." Her skin shone with sweat and her eyes with exhaustion and her pale face looked flattened out. Soon she ran out of words and stood there, the uncleanable apartment in a shambles around her—a two dollar strip of linoleum that was colored to look like a rug. "It's so painful when you just come and go. You don't stay, you don't say anything, you watch us and after a while you go again." But she gave up resisting and we rushed out and bought a bristly green tree and a bundle of presents, threw snowballs, and put on the radio for the carols, got benevolently drunk, and poor Tony had the kind of a day that he had much too often, a hectic heaped one which he was supposed to appreciate to the hilt, after the climax of weeping and tensions in which all the bones of the holiday had shown through—all the bones of the

grownups' needs, of which his enjoyment was intended to be the relief.

She showed me she made up his bed like an adult's, since he was in school, and showed me a plant he'd been given and a drawing he'd drawn. She talked about getting a job once he was old enough, when she'd get off Welfare and burn all her rags. Rags they were, too, a pitiful closet. I was brought up to date on everything, except hints were thrown out about new boyfriends in order to keep it all interesting. We talked through the weekend, Ida rooting for me wholeheartedly—my absurd boasts. Her mouth was like her accessible eyes, vulnerably wide, with a deep-set survivor's smile, a beautiful smile that probably owed part of its permanence simply to being such a large one. I loved looking at it while lying beside her, force-feeding her eyes. She was very acute but always the all or nothing type, and I was experimental. I had never been loved before and was somewhat the tyrant, or anyway fascinated by how variable women were, passion was so different from friendship. Her hair, if it wasn't limp, was lovely and springy. She had heavy long slick-skinned buttocks on rather short legs, sharp breasts. I hung a bathtowel on myself to show how potent I'd gotten. She said she was glad we had met while she still had some of her youth left to give me. Her cheeks, as wide as a cat's, could be middle-aged-sullen or wonderfully girlish. She had toil-ridden hands and a workhorse neck because she'd supported her family from the age of fifteen. She believed in the soothsaying stars as well as her dreams, the latter of which sometimes awed me. On the street, if I spotted her half a block down, she looked intimately linked to me like a relative, but all out of whack,

preoccupied, miserable. She lived such a hairtrigger life that she'd wait half the night by her door for me to come home when we'd fought, yet be far from amenable. And I played her the dirty trick of connecting her in my mind with the maids my family had had in my early teens whom I'd never got up the nerve to try and lay but had wanted to. It was especially dirty since she was so conscious of caste. She'd had to leave school to scrub people's floors, and she would have hated me.

Darwin, meanwhile, was fizzing along. He concocted electrical devices as well as his medical stuff. He was the kind whom one feels the sorriest for, where the energy's there but amounts to nothing. He set a room aside for Ohm's Law, with shelves that almost met in the middle and equipment that hummed from the floor to the top. He began buying equipment in earnest, having inherited a few thousand dollars from an uncle who had died in Colombia, and at once became secretive. This was the break that would bring the bonanza. Nights and Sundays he gave to the Law (Sundays his favorite day now), alone in the building except for the painters who had studios; and no love was lost among that bunch. Whenever you stayed in the building late you discovered new mysteries about the people. The fad was to buy camouflage cloth from the war surplus stores, so that, seen from the outside, the windows looked kooky and jungly.

The crazier a person was, the less tolerance he seemed to have for his neighbors, the less mercy or pity, and the harder he was to deal with. We had a woman we used to give leftovers to after lunch, but she wouldn't open the door no matter how loudly you called out her name. You had to put the food down, knock, and

then leave, making plenty of noise so she'd know you were gone. Garbagecan Maisie. Darwin was called Quasimodo by the painters and, in turn, was raucous about their dead ends. He called me Lad, which, feeling as green as I did, I didn't mind. In his wilder states I was Androcles, never suspected of plots against him. He *was* quite like Quasimodo, in fact; once I had heard the name I couldn't forget it. He was cheerful and singing much of the time, blinking and deaf to the outer world. I could see him up in a belltower kicking and pushing away at the bells. His own plots were hair-raising, involving his tubes of Tb as they did. Of course he never carried them out but I had my first taste of powerlessness listening to him, because if I'd phoned the Health Department it was I, not he, who would have been judged to be nuts. With his animals, while he was humane in the short-term ways like water and food, his experiments grew very probing.

At my window, being left to myself, I went through a knightly period. If I saw a colored lady unsuccessfully trying to persuade a taxi to stop for her, I would go down and signal one and hold the door open, so that the driver wouldn't realize that I wasn't the passenger until it was too late. And a muscular, rebel Negro in a wheelchair lived around the corner. He would need to go out for food or a bottle of liquor, hating to ask a favor, and yet there was no other way to get over the curbs. When he was sober you'd see him swallow his pride and do it, but if he was drunk he would spin in his chair in circles for fifteen minutes on the edge of the traffic, yowling and sobbing, as the people avoided him all the more. So I used to go down for that.

Darwin took to working far into the night and bought a cot to

sleep on at the office in the midday. Either he slept scarcely at all or he slept like a dead man, wildly irregular. He cooked for himself and cooked for his mice, and the smells combined with the hammering from the locked room (he was putting up still other shelves) was crazy. As always when he was most withdrawn, he looked his most clean-cut and pleasant. He quit joshing with patients, worked in silence, and contaminated some of the culture plates in his haste. He had laughed at the neighborhood's burglar alarms, which were always going off, ringing all night, but now he installed one himself. The work we were given fell off. I spent long lunches watching the *bocce* on Houston Street, more Italian that Italy, really, or walked to the library or to one of the kosher sandwich emporiums or, in the summer, to the public pool near Avenue C where upwards of a thousand children would be swimming and the universal shrillness was like sunlight. Long lines waited behind the diving board: two lifeguards stood ready. Each kid climbed on and walked to the end, every step broadcasting that he hadn't the faintest idea about how to swim. In he'd plop. The guards took turns going in. Sometimes, leaving the lab at night, I passed by the local high school and found the whole street spread with trumpeters blowing away, the very bleakness everywhere else accentuating the gaity. Postponing going home, I'd look through the paper for anything uptown to do. In the winter, if worse came to worst, I just sat in the subway where it was warm, reading the news with the men who dreaded going home to their wives. It was a year of intense wretchedness and happiness mixed, each deepening and giving the other color. On the subway, I amused myself by imagining that everyone sitting there was in armor of various sorts.

Ida's laugh became nearly as throaty when I kissed Tony as when I kissed her, since it was plain that I loved him a bit and that her hopes of marrying again weren't going to suffer because of her son. Her dependence made her even more of a hothead and made me take her for granted, besides. We avoided each other for days, despite his pathetic attempts to bring me back, when he'd knock at my door on his own initiative and tell me his mother wanted to see me, "needed" to (this after I'd heard her drunken yelling). But if we suddenly met, we'd get into each other's arms again, the sarcasms crackling, and her soft buttocks filling my hands. She'd lean her head back for a kiss. She compared her husband and me, both bastards, and laughed, "Has the dance palled?"—meaning her rivals. I'd never made so much love before, and found it was habit-forming. Success brought success. I chased, phoned, and dashed about, pushing, pushing defenses down, wet in the pants and wet in the mouth, this brimstone to her, naturally—the poor woman could hear the high heels through the ceiling if I brought someone in—I soon didn't. She'd upend her apartment and clean and explode, and the next day, hearing her yell at her son, I'd show up scared at her door for his sake, wondering who I should call. She asked who I was; had she met me before?

"You thump in here as if you're some king. Well you're not, you're just Johnny Average to me, and you better believe it. You're disgusting. You walk up and down those stairs—you're as arrogant as a turkey—I don't listen for you any more, you know. I'm not your biddy. You think he loves you. He doesn't love you. And I don't love you. I'm just curious to see what you'll come up with next. I learn, you know. I don't give a damn if a man like you drops dead in the street. You're just a fucker—yes, you're flattered, aren't

you, you're such a boy. You think that's a good thing to be. You love me to kiss your chest. You think it's such a magnificent chest, don't you? You think it gives me a charge."

When she didn't drive me out, she clutched at me like a life ring, and didn't hear a word she said, because if I left she hadn't a clue as to why but would stand with the tears slowly penetrating the glaze in her eyes. Holding each other, we watched Captain Kangaroo, who was such a slob that he was a comfort. Tony, letting his oatmeal congeal, stared funnel-faced too. My notion was that, regardless what happened between me and his mother, some day I would help to put him through college, or get him out to the country for summers. I hoisted him over my head, gulping down my delight in being a father; and the two of them lined up next to the door when I left for work to kiss me off.

Once she thought she was pregnant everything was intensified. She talked about Tony for hours, as though lonelier now, bored with romancing, only the mother. The round-robin trading of germs went on, like her crescendo-type suffering, standing past midnight behind the door. I felt horribly trapped. Why in god's name was I living down here? Half my attraction from her standpoint was because I came from another world. And why had I gotten myself in the fix—I'd forgotten how new the experience of winning love was. I'd made use of her and now it was nothing but castor oil pains and a sanity stretched to its limits. I was scared to death. She with her neat, small ears, French nose, and her scrub-woman's lumpy arms—at my dreariest, I could imagine us going through the clinic mill and the intern's glances directed at me wondering why. The battered old tenement faucets rang like

sleigh bells, and we were as merry as mourners, she sitting beside my knees. She hated men, worshipped men, and I rubbed her forehead, where the slamming she'd taken had registered most, the deprived and underdog bones. But she bloomed in exultancy, maneuvering her figure. She looked like a movie star. It was my baby. We were knitted together now. I was chilled to the bone! I'd never imagined such passion existed, much less that I might be the object of it.

When this aghast reaction of mine was clear, Ida got into more of a rage than anything else could have put her in. The luster went out of her skin. She turned into a fiery sick cat, bedraggled and humped. "Why didn't you let me alone? All right, we played house nicely and you found out you couldn't care less for the likes of me, I was beneath contempt; so why didn't you leave me alone? Why did you leave it up to me? It was so peaceful without you, I was getting along perfectly. But no, you wanted me on the string for the times when you hadn't anyone better. You revolt me, my friend. I don't want your baby. You figure out how to get rid of it. I haven't the energy to spare for you—I need what I have for my son." And, indeed, her efforts were all to shield him and keep up his routines.

Darwin puttered or pounded throughout the day in either his guinea pig room or his "juice" room, while Lafayette Street grew still grislier. Bums are straight out of a comic strip anyway, with their charcoal-smeared faces, their staccato-gapped teeth and gallows-bird postures that look like they've already been hung. When I watched a man chased down the street by a man with a

knife, it was slapstick, like the comics, not TV representationalism. In the first place, the knife was outsized, and the man in front completely the wrong shape for running, and the man following him, though less bloated, ran like his feet were in boxes, plus the outlandish pursuers who were trying their best not to catch up. Real street fights were broken up into whirring fragments with baby-like waaahs, and bums fought with wood slats like Punch and Judy—the outcries, the shadow-show fury—till, after a long inaudible speech, the winner would take a few theater bows. My troubles at home didn't help remove me. On the contrary, I lost my perspective, I could see only the suffering. When I was pipetting something, I'd distinguish a child's shrieks under the rush of the cars and look out the window and see one being whipped on the legs for minutes on end by her father. What could you do? To step in directly would make it worse for the child—the mother already was doing her best to distract him—and to call the police would be more drastic yet, once the guy talked his way out of it and got the girl home. The only weapon was simply to watch—to *watch,* so that the fellow knew. Long after the family had left, I would be jumping up from my desk to lean out with cramps in my chest as if it were still going on.

In the army I'd worried about being "dehumanized," although the army had softened me, but here was a vastly more brutal environment. The truck drivers shouted Giddyap at the bums pulling pushcarts. Even the street was caving in because some foundations had been misdug, and it threatened to block up the subway. I was just high enough to be out of throwing range if I shouted at people. When I was outside myself, though, I quickly got expert at looking away. Either you watched pointedly or, for

safety, you looked away. One time a troop of housewives and I followed four or five friends who were beating the wife of one of them, stopping and pulling her into doorways until our staring, our numbers, dislodged them.

Ida was shifting furniture to cause a miscarriage and doing hot baths. Going by on the stairs, I heard the brass ring to her voice, on the phone calling friends. After a minute she'd tap at my room to tell me the latest, since it was me in her body budding. Steaming with fear, she went up to Central Park and leapt off the boulders. My hair stood stiff to hear about it. I hugged her, begged, and yet finally had nothing to say, realizing how little the difference was between jumping off boulders and going to the doctors that Darwin knew. She was petrified; she said that her life was a wreckage; she felt hot to the hand as if she were running a temperature and could hardly put two words together, afraid that they might take Tony away, and frightening the daylights out of me. All of a sudden, however, worred that it was some cruel piece of egotism, I would look at her and be tremendously pleased at the pregnancy, sexually excited, and go over her with my hands. She felt the same way immediately. We made the most tender, delicious love, with her stomach the center of it, never so sexy.

Darwin considered me some sort of link to the rest of the world, and joked about "raping girls" and the rest of it, though disarmingly gentle. He told World War II stories, sitting across from me at his aluminum table and wiping his ribs with a towel if he wore no shirt. He liked to keep to a schedule, to overwork, which wasn't easy in a lab such as ours, and occasionally to take time off for an indulgent talk with me.

"I'll tell you, lead your own life. Nobody has any business with

you. They won't understand what you want to do. They'll laugh at you out of ignorance. So you don't ask permission from anybody when you pick out something you want to do, you just go ahead, and then you won't have any problems," he said, the brief phrases to add pithiness. But his successful man's manner was rendered incongruous by the misfit's tone, the schoolboy solemnity, he gave everything. It was in his mouse room that he could be bluff the most briskly. The hundreds of rustling creatures did seem like employees—another twill factory in operation. He inspected them with overseeing interest, or picking them up, injected their stomachs, their poor little pots, with that undeniable affection which experimenters, seeing them always as plural, have for their animals as a group.

Our peppiest moments came when a bold bum would wander in wanting his heart listened to. Darwin got shouty, but if the guy didn't run out of the office or wasn't insulted he usually would change around. He rapped his stethoscope affably into his hand like the doctor he'd wanted to be. He'd sit on the edge of the desk and chat like a boy with a younger boy, wrapped in smiles, not so puffy-faced now. These were his cheeriest periods of all, as if he realized that he could still be a part of the world. The bum inevitably blossomed out too, thought he was awfully skillful to get so much free attention—blood pressure taken—and even forgot his worries about his health. The loudest voices are the voices of bums. The final survival energies, drawn if necessary from everywhere else, seem to go to their throats. We had several memorable specimens, stuffed into their clothes like badly made puppets, the clothes brown and gray and all torn—stains, a scrap

of a beard. They were bodiless heads. They were so badly off the only reason they still could walk was that they had wasted away to nothing. But the voice mushroomed, as strange as the lush, unnatural plants which grow out of dead things. Or sometimes the only piece left of a bum was his laugh:

"Wherever I happen to be I'll come in for a checkup every few months, just to be on the safe side. I'll look-see if I can't see a fairly intelligent-looking doctor some place pretty close around. I don't like to walk too far away for it. That way you don't have to worry, you know nothing is sneaking up on you, and if you do what the fellow tells you to do you're gonna be okay until the next time—little heart murmur or something, it's gonna be all right. Oh I can take the cold, I'm very good on that. I know the techniques. They trained us with that. I was up on the DEW Line three years you know. I was up in the Arctic. A lot of these bums wouldn't last a day. Three years of that and you'll take the cold fine; you can take anything. Yeah, you'll see some snow up there, you'll see some dandy cold."

He was like a boy who was shining shoes, this one, with his pert line of gab and the patronizing smiles we gave him. He had hands like a turtle's skin, and strips of newspaper inside his socks, a red toucan nose, a white and red face like a ham bone, and he shook like a soaked sourdough from his illnesses. His ragged coat flapped in the wind like a flag when we watched him leave. Right away he begged from a car at the light, not to lose the boost to his confidence: he put hands carefully behind him and stooped like a bon vivant to speak to the driver.

We also watched the fences at the garage. I laughed but Darwin

was bitter like any respectable citizen under siege. It was hard to tell what was going on because they also worked at the regular jobs. They filled up the place with cars and sweated all day, with a reputation for piddling cheating. But then these cryptic vans would pull in, *Pong's Produce, Old Reliable Pipe and Joint*—ten-year-old trucks which had been painted over a dozen times. They'd move the whole garageful in order to stick the truck in the back, getting very excited and busy.

There is nothing likeable about criminals. They're sneering creatures, ready to turn vicious in an instant, and it was an exacerbation to have them placed opposite us. Of course it made little difference to them when I waggled my finger. They'd grab up tire irons and chase a man. If a Negro drove in for gas, they gave him a Queen Isabella bow and had him wait, pretending to be just about to come, in order to see how long they could keep him. "You goddam bow-and-arrow, get outa here!" They worked, they threatened, in absolute incoherence—a shrug, a lunge at the breastbone. They couldn't talk without jabbing their hands at the person, the mark of respect being not quite to touch him. My stomach got turgid and hot as I'd watch an incident develop. For some reason I went back to the screw-you signal of my boyhood and pointed with that, trying to make myself heard. I shook in confusion for the next half hour whether I'd stayed to watch the scene out or whether I'd ducked away like Darwin. They robbed their own pay phone when they needed change, and the Puerto Ricans hated them too and used to write "warps," "gunnies," on the wall at night after the place closed. One Sunday Darwin watched a car which they hadn't been able to fit inside completely

stripped, down to the axles, by three Negroes. He was delighted. It yawned there Monday, while the men fumed.

The four were related, I got the impression, except for a muscle-bound fellow who seemed the most decent. The dominant guy was a blast of straight vigor. He worked a twelve-hour day in his shirt sleeves into December, never ceasing to bluster and shout. He ate with his left hand and worked with his right, talking over his shoulder to the hired, muscle-bound one and yelling ahead to his fat husky brother. The brother, with an unpleasant face, kept up with his share of the jobs but sourly. He had the children who played nearby, attractive twins. The fourth man, who was maybe a cousin, was nervous-natured and thin and tall. He had lithe, precise hips that pumped when he walked. He was the most unpredictable and independent and had an oddly chic wife who came and sat in their car every few days while he worked. She looked nice; she was a softening influence, very much gentling him. A snide scowl snuck over him when he got the snow shovel and ran for a bum (they'd let the guy go in a corner and start to pee first). The two children did not have a dampening effect, but when his wife was around none of this happened. He resented me—he was the one who stared back. If I passed on the street he usually quit working sarcastically, though we never spoke.

Virgil Grissom and Hubert Humphrey were driven through on their way up from City Hall. We had a vegetable wagon clatter by daily that serviced the luncheonette downstairs. I looked down at the part in the horse's mane. The Hoodoos fought with the Roman Emperors in the next block. And we had Light and Gas

men. They were trying to pump out a manhole before doing some job, except that it filled up again every night. In the morning they strung tapes around the hole, hung warning flags, and set the pump going, and smoked and Coked the day away until the last hour, when they took everything down again. And a mailman made constant pickups—it has to be seen to be believed how many are made.

By the garage was a liquor store owned by a man with a villainous voice and a face shaped like smoke, gray as smoke, who flapped one hand smartly behind when he zipped along on a delivery. He parked in the station and was friends with the bunch, although he considered himself a cut above them. Ours was the civilized side of the street. Right below me was a classical tailor, who suffered like a sunfish in a pail; and, next door to him, a womanly printer whose window display had not been changed for fifteen years and whose mouth was as large as his stomach, the better to laugh with, presumably. He cut the ads for his son-in-law's business out of the paper and carried them around like snapshots. Then his cobbler friend, as skeptical and as seamed as a jockey. He hammered so neatly it was like a stage set: stroke, stroke, the sole was fast; and the nails in his mouth for comic relief. He had a comedian's mouth anyway, and he'd go out and pet the vegetable horse. Two Puerto Ricans ran the luncheonette in eager immigrant fashion. The best thing about them was how they walked off at six o'clock, rolling like seamen, relaxing so hard. They were agreeable and got along fine until the slap-dash cooking cut into their business. They responded by cooking more hastily still and by stinginess with the portions and reducing the menu, so that it was another sad story.

We had plenty of people around and yet we had nobody. When something happened and I would go down I would be on an empty street. In my way, I was expert at preserving my own skin. I never "closed" with anyone, just put myself close at hand. When a car jerked out of the traffic one time with screams from inside, I opened the door on the girlfriend's side to help her get out, not the man's, and retreated as he came after me. "Oh you better run, he'll kill you!" she shrieked. I could see Darwin's pale face above me, and the jockey squinted behind his window as if he were watching a dangerous jump. Darwin believed he had a sixth sense, which made him especially fearful. By now he was sure I'd get clobbered. He told oodles of war stories, remembering more as he went along, and displayed the scars of a beating he had received from some young homosexuals in an earlier phase. They'd tattooed the star on his hand, which alone would have made it impossible for him to return to a more normal life, he claimed. Breakdowns and other new chapters were revealed. An old anxiety about robberies returned. He stopped inviting his Spanish friends up because they might see the equipment and be tempted. He checked the door to the roof twice a day. "That's where they come, off the roof." While he was scared to sleep in the lab, he was even more afraid to leave it unguarded. He used army phrases, shaking his head and gritting his teeth. He even quit leaving our leftovers outside the old lady's door down the hall in case she broke in some night after more.

But he was *for* me, telling me twenty times that he would be my character witness. It was often the police I was battling. In civilian clothes a guy would march off a vagrant, refusing to show him his badge, just whacks. Or when they stormed in in response

to a call, arrowing down Lafayette the wrong way—these were the large, lengthy scenes, spreading across the wide street, repetitious but excruciating after you had seen a few. The gold-badges slapped with open hands, as a detective would. The silver-badges poked their clubs like bayonets until a pretext came for swinging down. I bought a camera and drafted letters to the *New York Times.* I fretted on the outskirts, trying to copy cap numbers, and more than once I only saved myself from being arrested by backing off. The standard ending became to find myself being forced to lay my ID cards across the roof of a police car while all the stuff was written down, to stand there, hands on top of the car, in front of the open door—it functions as a sort of station house—until the decision was made as to whether to arrest me or not.

I got nutty, no question about it—more compelled and susceptible, quick to tear and quick to tremble. My eyes had been rubbed raw. The fire escapes on the garment factories filled up with people if a Negro was involved, and some of them would rush downstairs and fuss with me on the edge of the action. My ragged nerves were like theirs. I had seen so much violence by now, so many atrocious injustices, that any beginning carried its whole plain progression for me—I understood Darwin's sixth sense. The police were the same, for that matter, and so were the gas station toughs. Everybody picked up from the last time. Anger from then, or anguish, whatever it was, piled onto the new occasion. In a flash the despair poured back, and I would be leaning over the patrol car hood again, my teeth practically chattering. "No, no sir, buddy, you take out your fucking license yourself! I don't handle nobody's wallet!"

It was December, that awful Christmas, and we had the procession of Santa Clauses coming out of the subway all day with their locked boxes and Santa Claus bells. Their terminus was a mission on Houston, so we had the entire city's street Santas, who were really just ordinary bums dressed up in red and white, limping along much as usual—they didn't bother with stomachs for them. We also had Fire Department exercises going on within a couple of blocks. I needed a vacation badly, needed to get to the country; I was irritated simply by humans and human activity by this time. If a bus driver reached the end of his route and wanted to turn around, I argued with him. The signs on a church or a synagogue that said that it closed at 8 p.m. struck me as pharisaism. At my cheerfulest I typed myself with the bearded, anachronist Jews in shiny black coats, only a very few left, who still hauled their pushcarts through all this madness in the old style, purple with sweat, having no relation whatever to it.

Though the frog tests I did on Ida continued to run negative, she wouldn't menstruate and the doctor thought that he felt a pregnancy rather than cancer—he said it was *something*. I would drop in on the way to work, if possible, because of my own shakiness, instead of at night when I would have to stay longer. I gave her money and horrified hugs and pained, gingerly looks which tried to convey affection. It's hard to reconstruct exactly what she was feeling since I was trying to avoid being aware of it. She "suspected" I didn't love her, though of course I believed I had never pretended to; and she really thought a good deal of the time that she was going to die or at least be made sterile. She dreamt of water, of babies, of me, of death, and raged against being a

woman, while at the same time she was trying to shield me from what she was going through, that is, except for the nights when she heaped her sufferings on me in blinding half-hour explosions, her voice like a flatted cornet. She ate and threw up as if she were pregnant, and looked taut and scrawny with that violin-string attenuation of a cat which drags itself. Then, next morning, what a Liz Taylor opened the door, bellying gay as the clouds! I'd bite her. I had a permanent cold from exhaustion.

Her room and a half had her marriage furniture in it, appropriately mismatched and in faded bright mummylike colors. When there wasn't another reason, my heart went out to her for the apartment alone, so unspeakably dismal and small, and she without even the subway fare to get out. The layers of paint and linoleum extruded dirt from tenancies fifty years past. The two beds took most of the space. The books were her husband's Genet, the decorations her own sporadic attempts which she couldn't get rid of when the mood left until she saved enough money to buy something else. I regarded the place as mine for loafing ("your doll house," she said), and we still had rather happy, whimsical evenings sometimes, with billing and cooing, no barbarities. We lived on three different planes, mine being the mundane. Ida was in a shadow world, smelling life, smelling death, the surface realities scarcely a glimmer part of the time. She drew upon every ounce of her concentration to manage the details of Tony's existence, yet he chirped out the window obliviously. He had the most marvelous shrieks and chirps, like nothing I'd ever heard before. I almost wanted the baby born. He shot with his gun out the window too much and chased the cat hard, had very pitiful

moments, but mostly one wondered whether he wasn't living on borrowed time, whether such glee in defiance of logic and of his surroundings wasn't going to have to be paid for. Certainly in other respects he could go either way. He was slummy-faced, coarse and tough for a while, as if growing up to be somebody I wouldn't be able to care about. Then in the afternoon, maybe, his eyes would spread open, his face would go soft, as he listened to one of his mother's tales of Aesop. He was precociously gentle whenever she reached her rope's end, just as Ida after an incendiary couple of hours always stopped short and knelt down in order to make it up to him with an effusion of playful intuitive love.

Twice the social worker dropped by unannounced for what was called a Complete Drawer Count. And the tenement pipes rang like railroad bells. "Just hold onto me," she'd whisper, as crazy as eels. It was "*Please* don't stare!" or else "You're not looking at me!" when I was too anxious and pitying. The truth, as we waited for word from the doctor to act on, was that the danger that she'd have a breakdown was worse than the risk of any abortion. She was Catholic, and I rubbed her resisting back by the hour while she talked. I was a futile substitute, but she was afraid she'd lose Tony if she went to a priest, and she made me afraid to go to one too. Listening, I couldn't fix on a plan for any of the eventualities. There were other shouts in the building but not pitched like hers, and she lay with her head in my lap, so that I saw the tears in her nose and the swollen blood vessels. Tony writhed on the floor.

"I've taken so much and what have I got to show for it? I have you here, younger than me, almost a child really, because you were

hard up, and now you like to think of yourself as wonderfully kind and honorable. I don't care who's with me. I don't even know where I am. Have you ever felt neuter? Well that's how I feel. I don't feel like a man and I don't feel like a woman. I'm dead, I'm an idiot, I don't feel. I wish I were a tree, or have I read that somewhere? I must have. Nothing is original with me, is it? I don't believe in God but I'm afraid of Him. I don't particularly like you, but I loved you—that's not original either. I don't want to sleep with any more men or have any more babies but I don't want to be sterile. I see horrible figures in dreams, but they're the best company I have except for my son. I'd do anything not to die, but I want to die."

Just as dreaming of having a breakdown is said to tap off the pressure building towards one, when the janitor in our building cracked up Ida appeared to revive, to catch a kind of a second wind. It was a hectic long night. The guy was afraid his relatives were going to kill him and begged for help in heart-rending yells, but he was the one who was armed and they were only afraid for their lives. He ran into the tenants' rooms for protection, and when we ran out, he followed, afraid to be left by himself. With his knives in his hands, he went down on his knees and begged us to spare him.

Soon we were to find out she wasn't pregnant at all, but I'd sunk into a state where my laughing and joking were of no use. I couldn't eat. I was worn out, bewildered and worthless as far as assisting her was concerned, and unable to pick myself up or take a sensible trip or take some good pills. There had been no chance to collect my wits and hunt uptown for a job. I thought I'd never get

out of this, and the winter shut most people indoors, so that the suffering seemed that much worse. If you dodged past a barefoot beggar, the blood on his face had froze. The old Jews took temporary respites, but the bum pushcart pullers continued wretchedly. Many drivers hardly acknowledged their right to the street anymore, so long after the heyday of pushcarts.

It may have been an impatient attempt to scare the man or a misjudgment because of the novelty. Maybe the cart didn't register on the truckdriver's eyes, being neither a pedestrian nor a motor vehicle. Barreling along and simply not seeing it, he clipped the cart from the rear, spinning the man in front of him. He didn't begin to brake or swerve until it was done. We called the police from upstairs. Darwin had bought some goldfish and was tinkering with the aeration. By now it was established he never was going to go down on the street if something was happening; and I didn't object; I didn't want to go either. But I'd seen the accident. The man was lying there with nobody touching him, and I still had a sense of being "medical": in fact appeals on those grounds were occasionally made to our window.

He looked dead from close up. I asked in the liquor store if we oughtn't to phone for an ambulence. The fellow was doing paperwork.

"Nobody can call an ambulance except the cops. You know that. What's the matter with him?"

"He was hit by a car," I said. I'd disliked his preposterously sinister face for so long; he turned round and grinned.

"Yeah? Well probably you ought to call the cops, don't you think?"

I was unable to answer that. Outside, I looked up and saw Darwin worrying in the window, as were the printer and the two Puerto Ricans on our side of the street, although they had no apparent reason for worrying about me. A nervous tick in my cheek asserted itself; I realized I was bone-tired.

"Phone for an ambulance," I yelled to Darwin. The victim appeared quite decidedly dead, however. For all the illness I'd seen, he was my first dead man, and yet since he looked like hundreds of magazine pictures—the ragged refugee dead by the road—the sight could not have been more familiar. Every night going home I went by at least one drunk passed out, usually in danger of freezing. Dead as they looked, I went by assuming, like everyone, that somebody else was going to stop, because to see to them would have tacked on an hour or more to my day. This was absolutely routine, but I felt for a pulse with a sadness that had a momentum behind it—he *was* dead, I knew. Sick, shaky, I wanted to laugh. The pity I had withheld so many times had caught up with me. The traffic streamed by. A couple of the gas station men came out to wave it on so that their entrance wouldn't be blocked, and the truck driver passed cigarillos around. He was very upset, an outspoken, balding person in a checked wool jacket. It was after four, nearly dusk.

"They shouldn't be let on a street like this. I mean it's for stuff that's going through, you're supposed to go around twenty-five, thirty-five miles an hour. Poor baby. That never happened to me before. Right out of the blue, they step in front of you and you've killed somebody. Poor bastard. Jesus." He walked around between us. I didn't nod to agree but, on the other hand, didn't find him

objectionable. The difficulty was that I had an exact image of what I had seen. As crisp as a diagram, the truck had traveled in a straight line. The cart had been in the path of that line and at no time had the truck hesitated. The impact with the man was too searing to bring to the front of my mind but it was indelibly there. The daylight, dim to begin with, was rapidly vanishing.

I went up to the lab, since I could feel myself get incoherent. The man was dead; no sense in gawking about. "Oh, all bashed to hell, that's all." I told Darwin. "Hit him from behind." The truck had *McMartin's Scotch Whiskey* on it and a pasteboard bottle, and the driver, we saw, walked into the liquor store and provoked enough interest that the proprietor at least poked his head out the door. The Texaco bunch toed the cart frame. "Vamose," they said to a carload of Spanish, keeping the driveway clear.

From the gestures, a consensus was forming by which the pushcart man was to blame. Nobody checked him again, and I wondered if I hadn't been too quick in presuming him dead. Though this was nonsense, I came down. They were by the truck, looking for damage. Without much basis, I got the idea the guy might have handed out a few bottles as I was coming downstairs. The cart man, in Raggedy-Ann clothing, was partly thrown on his side, with his head bloodied and his seat all cut up from a bottle of wine that had been in his back pocket. Amazed, I recognized him as the one who had sat and chattered to us about the DEW Line in such an incongruously lively way. All of that spunk and spark smashed up like a broken doll—it revolted me.

"They shouldn't let them out on the street, or you'll even see them up on the sidewalk. No light on him, no way to see him,"

the driver complained. The others wanted to drag the cart over a bit to let the traffic pass by faster. "Leave it. It's way the hell out there," he said. But with a scared, guilty face like mine might have been, he swung back to me as if I was the one he wanted to convince because I was next to the body.

"Nevertheless he was on the street," I said.

"'Nevertheless?'" He sounded the word, mixing respect and sarcasm. "What are you, a doctor?"

"No he's not a doctor, he's just a Nosy," chuckled the thin mechanic. I'd always been glad it wasn't one of his huskier partners who had taken the special dislike to me, but I saw he could beat me up easily.

"I knew him a little," I said.

"You knew him?" Bolder, the driver asked with his eyebrows *why* I knew him. I hunched by the body, feeling righteous and safe. After walking off, he came back and stared down at the man in sad disapproval. He leaned with a nervous snort, touched the man's rear, and smelled the alcohol on his finger. "Maybe the noise frighened him." His hands did the noise, then the cart veering into the traffic suddenly. Charades over drunks were so commonplace, one had to remind oneself that this fellow was dead; and—although I was glancing for suspicious bulges on them—the way the garagers were looking at me, I might have been the man who had run the bum down.

"I knew him, yeah." The store owner left his doorway. "All the bums around here." He puckered his mouth, looking down, as if to convict any customer of his. The driver asked who delivered his liquor to him.

Why was I being so punctilious? I'd sympathized with the driver at first—why get him in serious trouble when nothing constructive would come of it? The man would be just as dead. In the same way as the gas station crew had taken his side partly to spite me, wasn't my attitude the reverse? With their long-flanked red faces and their choo-choo-choo vigor, I'd never seen them so close before. It was like bars being removed. Here they were next to me, no barriers. And they all had the camaraderie of living in Queens and shaking their heads at the neighborhood. The dynamic, blocky, all-vigor guy kept leaving to heave himself onto the fender of the *Pong's Produce* truck and practically disappear inside its motor. "You live in that place?" he asked me, pointing.

"I work there."

"You work there?" He laughed at the building facade with its blotchy camouflage curtains and the wreaths around *MARY*.

"I'm a medical laboratory technician," I said, trying to invoke the immunity more than the prestige.

"Where do you live?"

They listened, these people I had been pointing at, judging and needling for months. It was too late to leave and I saw that by staying here to argue this issue I had lost whatever effectiveness I had been having up in my window. It was like the police interrogation would be. When they heard where I lived they guffawed.

The cart had carried junk cardboard, ground almost to powder by now, and pedestrians pumped by as thick as the cars. By standing still I got the sensation of managing some kind of show. The most touching detail was a handful of wooden letters the size

of a child's blocks, O's and H's, which were strewn alongside the gutter. In warm weather the cart must have been used as a hot dog wagon.

"Tell me something. Why are you all the time sticking your hand out the window? Are you trying to make a U-turn?"

We all laughed. The all-vigor fellow pushed up on his arms from the *Pong's Produce* motor to hear it repeated. A postman in a truck made a pickup, dragging his sack past the body. Infuriated that I was trembling, I searched for the top of the bottle, thinking that if the seal was still on I might prove the man had been sober. The early darkness was very confusing.

Once the cops came it was the trial in advance, acquittal quickly a certainty. They copied the license number on the tail of the cart. They shared with the gas station people that extraordinary beefiness found in the city. The owner of the liquor store emerged to touch the victim's rear end and convey the idea that he had been drinking, and the expression on the dead bum was no help. Besides being so very surprised-looking, he looked haughty and quarrelsome compared to when he had chattered to us about Hudson's Bay. It was the face of a man with freezing wet feet, with scarlet, goose-pimpled hands and neck, who was trying to ignore the shouts from the traffic and ignore his misery. When I drew my mind back to those moments before he'd been hit, I remembered no drunken appearance. He'd pulled like a dutiful, suffering horse that knows that its work is the lesser of evils. Now he looked like a crunched guttermouse made up for the role of a bum, with the stubble and stock ruby nose.

"Old bums like that, they don't carry a light, can't hardly

control what they're pulling, and they turn their ankle or they slip where it's wet—had a little too much—and out he goes in the lane. It's a crime when they're out like that," said the thinner garage man.

"Actually, the light was pretty good then," I argued in a despairing tone to the police. "I work right across the street, and he was coming down very fast, right by the curb. The poor guy was right in front of him. I don't think he ever did see him. It was much lighter than this, plenty of light. He didn't have his headlights on, himself, as a matter of fact, so it doesn't make any difference if the cart had a light of its own because it wasn't dark enough yet to need one."

Hoots from the witnesses. The scorch-faced owner of the liquor store said, "No, he had a load on."

The driver glanced over to where he was parked. "Well I turned 'em off, naturally, but I had 'em on, they were on."

"Sure, his lights were on."

I was chilled by the gas station group, for whom until now I had been pretty much of an abstraction, up in an upper story. They were giving me total attention. The stream of Santas climbed out of the subway, limping by us, and the ambulance came; another mail pickup was made. When the body was gone it required an effort to remember there even had been a body. As in the rehearsal, when they talked to me the police turned to look at my building. With their faces trained neutral, they asked how I'd seen through the camouflage cloth.

"I'm a medical laboratory assistant. We don't have that. We have the sign about blood tests in the window."

My home address registered badly again, as it would have in court, and perhaps I hammered too hard at the light being so good. Also, their first impression of me was marked by my searching look as to whether we'd crossed swords before, a look which must often betray petty criminals—that and the way I dropped my head like an exhausted bull in the ring, very small, windedly quivering. The uniform looked different to me. That charcoal blue—business blue. It had become almost impossible for me to talk to police without being hostile or supercilious, and so it was like a job interview, where my name was being written down but I knew I would never be hired.

I left work right afterwards, in a tumultuous funk. The killing, the codger gabbing away happily in our office only the week before, and everybody's closing over the facts of the accident—I felt as if I had flu. Darwin seemed queer as a coot with his star on his hand and his goldfish and mice and heavyweight name, and I wanted out.

As I crossed the Lower East Side, the record stores blared, the peddlers' trucks jingled, mocking me with a storm of sounds. A priest in an overcoat walked up and down on Elizabeth Street since he hadn't a cloister, holding a flashlight over his breviary and whispering the words. Kids were clouting a ball. They towered it up seven floors, then tried to spot it before it fell. A cat was making love to a dog. The light was so mutedly rich in night colors that my eyes led a life of their own. The vivid neons had a handmade gleam more stimulating than neons uptown, and the squint I'd developed, the squint of a person who couldn't walk five or six blocks without seeing a man slugged, an arrest or a beggar,

widened out in spite of itself. My eyes crowed. I heard Hindi, Rumanian, Cantonese, Polish, each lilty. A guy was thocking an oud with a spoon. Two beatniks had hung a piece of cardboard on their fire escape to communicate with the girl opposite—"Hey, Sweet!" Children spilled whooping across the sidewalk, and the off-Broadway theaters seemed like opera houses up in the Yukon, dowdy, primitive structures, newly white-washed, in the midst of a wilderness boom.

In my block the bookie's bird store had become bona fide. His life's enthusiasm was these evenings, when he really sold birds and sunflower seeds. He sat on a bin in his pigeon coop engulfed in wings, while he talked through the wire to a couple of pals. The whole block was dream-like and misty, the light Parisian, with every building a different color and height and shape, the fire escapes zig-zags of rusted orange, and the rooftops running along in a dum-de-dum-dum. Now I was squinting against the beauty—I must not be strong enough to live here. I caught a glimpse of two fencers upstairs in a loft, and a man inside a locked girdle store was playing his fiddle to a macaw. I looked at the lemons in the street stalls, at the mounded-up oysters and booties and Preen, feeling utterly flattened. That Ida's future should depend upon what I might choose to do was the worst circumstance of all.

She was plenty crazy at first that night: acute concentration on me. Her squeeze when we hugged was too strong to have any meaning as such and had none of the sexiness that was best at arousing concern.

"Something happened?" she asked. She was stroking my back to loosen it. With her harrowed face, which was so much more

anxious on my behalf than anyone else's would have been, she looked at me with an open love that overwhelmed me in shame, that she should be sorry for me, tenderly reading my muscles for tension, after the way I had dodged in and out the last weeks. A large face, like a boy's from medium range, like a woman's if you were close or away several yards. Brown eyes, black sweaty hair, and that great wide survivor's smile of hers, as serene as a smile in death. I got a fresh sight of this gritty girl who was carrying a child by me and living on powdered eggs and charity clothes and plain lonely terrified misery. I realized how little I'd done, how execrable it would look to me in a few years if I hadn't shut out the memory altogether. My god, how little I'd given her! Beer to help her relax at night? Not usually, unless we were necking. Blueberries, avocado, if I was having them? No, not unless we were eating together. A forkful of buttered string beans would have given her pleasure sometimes. I must have been mad—her son standing between my knees looked at least twice his age because of the life they were leading—I'd lost perspective completely!

I ran out and got mushrooms, steak and oregano and so on, and spoiled the meal only by hardly talking. Tony wanted the fathering element of it in equal proportion with the food, so he sat on my lap to eat, which he did with politeness and dignity. It was a funny meal. My affection for him gushed up until I could scarcely swallow, watching his every move, and with Ida I was the penitent husband. I'd forgot how at home we could be, although she assumed my silence was because of her pregnancy. But her glance lost its glaze; she got peaceful and sweet. She drew the big circles under my eyes with her finger.

"You've had a worse time, haven't you? You've worried more. You're very generous. Yes, you are," she said when I shook my head. "And I'm not after you, you know, that's not what I want, you mustn't feel any pressure like that." At her simplest and most attractive, she went on about how nice I'd been. She meant it, but at the same time I was thinking that we were half married already, and how fine it was to have supper this way, that to go through the further formalization might be right for me too. Once she was given a little stability, there would be just her warmth, no jaggedness. I couldn't bear picturing the boy dragged off to an orphanage, and felt protectively head-of-the-house. I began reaching under the table, and told her the accident story, more detached about it than I would have imagined an hour before. We hurried the dishes, mouth to the sweater already, and got Tony to sleep. She was a bit gaspier than I liked but very giving. Small breasts with large nipples, and an overall skinny toughness I loved—geisha-small feet with high arches, a mouth like a plum. It was another night when the loops bound around us made us relish each other all the more.

The next day we found out the loops didn't exist. I stayed home from work to get over the pushcart episode and she came in at noon from the doctor's and said he had made up his mind it was a false pregnancy. The explanation was skimpy because we had paid out so much already she didn't pay to have a long conference; but we scarcely hugged once after that. I left the house in blank angry relief and didn't go near her apartment for almost two weeks. I sought out a Negro girl I'd been flirting with, to enter that brittle, tight little set, the dark half of which wanted to go up in the world

and the white half of which wanted to go down. Since I, of course, wanted to go up like the Negroes, I didn't quite fit at the parties. She was the life and direction at them. She was impatient, tense, prickly, a virtuoso with people. We had one banner day, plus three club-foot attempts to repeat.

That district absorbed me all over again. I wandered as I hadn't since first arriving. Moist, smothery late December weather with wind and sun, when winter hovered just overhead, giving one more day's grace, now another. I got the exuberant sense that here in one spot was my whole fellow family of man. The racial mix on the streets brought a racial peace which was affecting if you went into other parts of the city. For both colors the process was rather like learning to fly—so many thousands of hours of looking to be put in—and down here we'd gotten farther along. Avenue C had a small-town flavor. Because of the cobblestones and the loose babies, traffic crept; the pedestrians virtually ignored it, so that there was a vacation atmosphere. I used to go into the Siberia Branch of the Merger Trust Bank for the fun of looking at who was assigned there. This was a grotesquely ancient building across from a live poultry market and a garment ends warehouse, and the tellers were dazed from their banishment from Madison Avenue. Italian ices had been sold out of baby carriages by Puerto Ricans during the fall, and practically every block had its *shul.* A *shul* was a hole-in-the-wall synagogue with four or five Stars of David built into the front, looking defiant and jubilant, from some ghetto in Europe and bursting with hope. In the zany designs of a lot of the blocks you could see the failed architects who at last had been left a free hand; they sometimes went Moorish to celebrate.

The neighborhood was as rich historically as the Range West of the same period, but was being bulldozed away. I strolled and gazed through the misty weekends—at the patchworks of relic wallpaper on the sites half demolished, at the washlines, the three downtown bridges—snacking on Old Country foods, and talking such talk as one enjoys slightly wistfully with a cab driver in more affluent years.

At the lab I tinked tunes on the urine bottles, lining them up. I treated the test frogs to beef liver for having been right about Ida from the start. Darwin was chiseling holes for a new wiring system. Five months instead of five years seemed the prognostication for him. He was eating graham crackers gobbed with butter ("I can't stop") and got bigger and bigger, more like an overblown boy of fourteen. The woman whose door we left the food at was also taking a turn for the worse. Twice she let her sink run until it overflowed. When we picked the lock we discovered her sitting in bed with her feet drawn up under her, watching the water. She creamed her skin and dyed her hair yellow, so it was hard to tell if she were senile or out of her mind.

I understood Darwin's fondness for mice. If you look at them they're graceful and comely. You can see them as panthers, you can see them as pandas. They cluck like a muffled henhouse, whereas guinea pigs sound like puppies down in the cellar. Light as a leaf and taut-legged, they skittered about their cages and sneezed from the bits of sawdust stirred up. They scratched their ears and cleaned their tails nattily and basked upon piles of each other as on piles of cushions, holding a nibble of food in their paws. Given food, they'd hurriedly wash their faces before feeling ready to eat,

and when they were hunched on their hams, their shoulders bulged out like extra pouch cheeks. Their tails were their pride and spiritual spine; they always were handling them, bending them round to clean and inspect. Stiff, up-curved tails signaled a fight; or a nervous mouse, with kissing noises, vibrated his tail out stiff and straight. After endearing, midget yawns, they often slept in a row like suckling pigs, and pressed their paws against their cheeks. Or they burrowed head first in a pile so that just their fat rears and pink, bird legs and rubber-hose tails stuck out. As they sickened, their white tails zoned into gray; they sagged and wizened like little sand bags. Sometimes they fled death in leaps, so that it clenched them in mid-air and they thudded down. Sometimes they lay on their sides, scrubbing their noses in spasms and coughing and sneezing, and went rigid like that, rolled up in the pose in which they'd been born and scrubbing pulsating nostrils. But it was generally a homey, humming room. Darwin and I often went in there.

My problems were solving themselves. If I was too scared to quit my job, the job was foundering under me. Obviously there would soon be no job. Although I was still at my window and my preoccupation with the violence got worse, I didn't dash down to the street so much. I avoided knots of the Harlem Negroes who worked near us, and would break into sweats of fear at odd moments, walking through a dark block—I developed a whiz-along walk. The subway was more than ever like an armed camp and, when I came out, I would see everybody facing in one direction and a man there trying to box with a bus. One day a cement truck stopped revolving. Rather than funny it was

frenetic. The driver cried. I'd gotten infallible at sensing a fight, sensing its start and exactly its course. Seeing people clumping in front of me, I'd usually turn off but sometimes I kept numbly on through the thick of it as if mesmerized.

The garage crowd amused itself by setting off left-over firecrackers from the horde they'd blackmarketed during the summer. They were having a lazy spell and would hire a passing bum to do some of their chores for a quarter or so. Ida was jumpy with me once our Christmas reunion was over, and Tony, taking his cue, was also cool, and yet we remained a threesome. He'd run away from me but then when I caught him and lifted him up he hugged me even as he was struggling. Ida was furious at my treating her like a taboo object. She moved away as if not to let me touch her any time I came close. Although I couldn't conceive of sleeping with her after the suffering that we had gone through, her person still seemed as much mine as a wife's. I refused to stay out of her room when she dressed. I pinched her elbows to see what she weighed and if she was eating enough. I touched my tongue to her forehead if she looked pale to feel what her temperature was. I used to rub her whenever we talked—rubbed and rubbed. I'd spank or order her around, give gifts as usual, fondle and advise her son—everything except sleep with her. Now that her life wasn't a shambles, wasn't about to break apart, she was left with it, which was not very pleasant either. It was a precarious, temporary sort of friendship we had, both of us riding along until I would go my way.

January was uneventfully dreary. The boiler next door blew up and ours at home went on the blink for a week out of sympathy.

One afternoon, at work, late again, about six, I heard the electric-horn blast, "You goddam spear-carrier!" A bum hadn't washed a car well enough but wanted his money. I winced at the window, it was all so familiar. The four mechanics were cutting across the lot in diagonal paths, toward the man or away after their monkey wrenches. The wife of the thin one was in the station, so he was trying to subdue his cousins a little, walking slower than them, waving his hand. The fellow was standing his ground on the theory that perseverance would carry him through. Standing quietly, he wasn't easy to see because his color just matched the shade of the darkness, his clothes showed up better. He was dead still. You had to look twice. He was only about in his forties, and everything happened very fast. When he saw the crowbars, he used language too. I was violently agitated. My face had lurched into a flinch; I'd stopped breathing. I was so clocked into the gears of this kind of stuff that every part of my body went sick as if as part of an allergy attack—I knew, I knew, I moved like one of the gears myself.

I was tearing downstairs. Outside, the whites were already in a half moon around the guy (the wife in the office door). "It was a shit, nigger job. You don't get nothing for that," said the blast-vigor brother with the voice like a highway horn. He had really too much energy to focus it on the one guy. The fat brother slouched in a posture of venom, but the muscle-bound hired man was less interested in hurting someone than in being strong. My lean opponent was between, holding them off as he cursed in an undertone for the Negro to run. In harassment he pointed at me as if "look what was coming."

"I done a good enough job. You weren't paying nothing but chicken feed anyhow. What do you want? You want to gyp me," said the man. He muttered that slavery wasn't going on any more. Not young, not quite humbled down into middle age, he was in the galled period of life when he had no impulsiveness left to save him. They encircled him, seeing how he took it, poking at his calves with a tire iron, and they called him one or two names. The auto trunks where they kept their weapons gaped open sinisterly. I'd drifted to the edge of the sidewalk on my side of the street with my tentative gait, my quick-backtrack gait, which had saved a great many necks by this time, including my own.

"I done a good job for you and you're going to keep my money?" He hadn't determined upon defiance, it was just happening. "What a poor sack of fish you are. You're cheapskates. Go on back to your tiddle-prick then. Go play with yourselves."

A moment went by before they could believe their ears. As one man, they turned and rushed for the woman, roaring, to drive her inside. The circle opened for that, but he still wasn't running; it was written into the lines of his body that he wasn't running. I'd never been faced with a situation where there was no running, so all my gingerly jumpiness was no help to me. I was picking my legs up and putting them down, twitching them almost like some sort of tail, but nevertheless remained frozen right where I was. I was nothing, unable to cross the street, unable to function. When they came back their feet shook the pavement, and a visible panic pushed up through his knees. The lean mechanic pointed at me to hold me where I was, and it was as though I were pressing against a thick pane of glass. The fellow did try to escape but had waited a

second too long. They ran him into the wall and held him there tight, waving their shovels and irons. "Call the cops! Call the cops!" they were yelling to Musclebound, in order to establish that they had phoned first and that an attack on them by the Negro had followed Musclebound's call. He shoved a dime in the phone, beating on it. I could see the white faces like flowers behind me in our building's windows. It was closing time; most of the lights were off; the cobbler was getting into his coat. I think I was yelling—at least my mouth was open. The Negro had covered his face with his hands. Since he didn't try to dodge loose, they didn't hit him more than a couple of times. I was weeping with the collapse of my nerves and because I'd done nothing; I'd been unable even to move.

The police dispersed all of us, finally. I was shaking and finished with this. After spending a few days at home sleeping, drinking milkshakes, I called up an uncle of mine in the midwest and borrowed enough to move uptown and devote myself to making a different start in the city.